TENERIFE TALES
With a twist in the tail
by Tony Thorne MBE

Introduction

Tony Thorne has the mind of a scientist and the soul of an artist. His science and technology are correct, his extrapolations wonderful and ingenious. But then – surprise! A blackness may descend – or a brilliant flash of black humour. Read and enjoy ...

Harry Harrison (Barcelo Varadero Hotel, 19.11.2007)*

**Harry Harrison is the celebrated American author of dozens of novels, and many collections of short stories. His books have been translated into over 30 languages. He visited Tony in Tenerife, for a warm sunny week, in 2007 and hopes to come again.*

TENERIFE - Tall Tales with a Twist
A collection of speculative stories.

First edition
ISBN 978-1-4092-0854-9

Acknowledgements

At the time of compiling, the following stories have previously been published, but only in earlier versions. i.e.

Long Term Survival, Formula 1 Extra, Hidden Recall, Hologhosts and ***Salvage*** - in ***Future Reassured*** - by Etcetera Press 2004.
Baggage and ***Retirement Plan*** - in ***Future Uncertain*** – by Etcetera Press 2005.
Informal Conversation – in ***The Romance Rag*** (USA) 2002.
Inside Information – in ***Second Opinion*** – *by* Etcetera Press 2005.

Dedication

Thanks to my liebe Wienerin Eva, and all my friends, present and past, in Tenerife; not forgetting Harry Harrison for his guidance, generosity, and most excellent company, during his last visit to the island.

TENERIFE TALES

A collection of short, and some longer, speculative stories.

Author's Introduction

This book is a collection of unlikely, speculative, yarns written on my portable **Neo** *word processor; during idle moments, either on the island, or when I'm thinking about being there ... which is often when I'm not!*

As a long time Science Fiction and Macabre Fiction fan, I'm well aware of my reputation as being some kind of nutcase for indulging in such activities. This being the opinion of some of my past and present friends, and even some relatives, who rarely indulge in such a strange pastime as reading the stuff; or even visiting a multiplex cinema, where more and more block-buster examples of the genre can be experienced almost every week.

Once I became a full time engineering business manager, which also entailed writing endless technical papers and reports, I never seemed to have the time to write fiction. Before I emigrated from the UK, to become absorbed in travelling the world on international business for an American Corporation, I did manage to pen a few examples, which were published, but nothing more until recently

Now, semi-retired, and spending as much time as I can in Tenerife, I've found the inspiration, and have the time, to pick up where I left off; too many years ago. My motivation is to introduce new readers, world-wide, to the literature I love, and not only visitors to Tenerife, where these tales are mostly located.

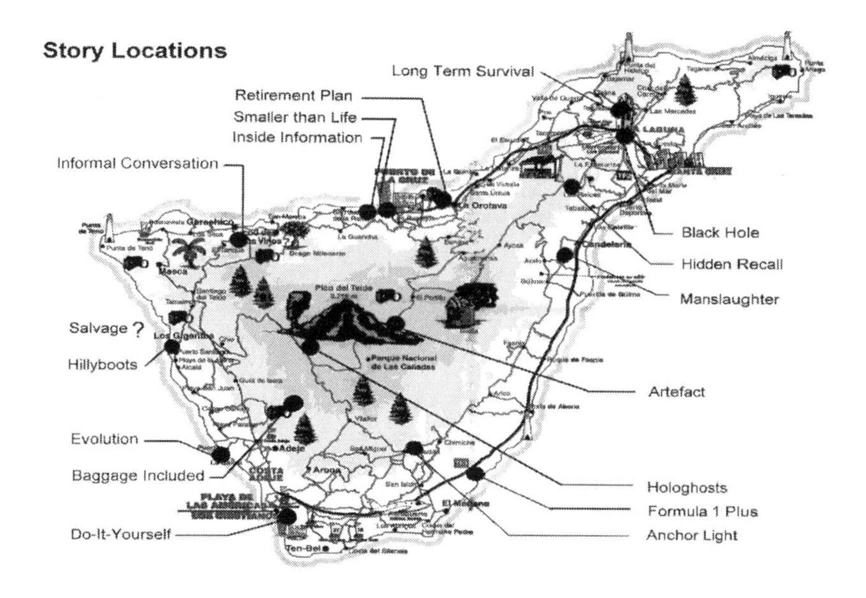

Page **CONTENTS**

This first unlikely tale does not actually take place in Tenerife, but parts of it do start there, and maybe more of it will later.

SMALLER THAN LIFE

The lone free-lance reporter, hovering around the speaker, was listening avidly and eager to hear something sensational to exploit. Herr Professor Kurt Pettermann was adamant, however.

“Please do sit down, I can only give you a few minutes, seeing how persistent you’ve been, but I want to stop these crazy rumours right now. There's no way we intend to clone any full size dinosaurs. That idea is ridiculous; we'd never be able to feed them.”

The reporter was disappointed. She sighed, closed her notebook, then stood up and exclaimed. "So what are you people going to do then?"

The professor smiled, confidentially.

"Fortunately we've discovered a way to genetically modify a creature's DNA, such that its size and growth is totally controlled. Our calculations show that the largest of the creatures we plan to select will not grow to be more than a few centimetres in height."

The relieved reporter sat down abruptly, opened her notebook again, and began to make some notes, as the professor continued.

"Impregnating the eggs will be tricky though, they'll be very tiny, but we have the necessary micro-handling tools designed and about ready for use."

"What are you going to use for a host, crocodile's eggs?"

"No of course not, they'd be much too large. We have a supply of eggs from the smallest species of lizards that inhabit Tenerife, in the Canary Islands. Even they are larger than we really want, but we believe they'll suffice. That's all I can tell you for now.”

The reporter had been saving, what she hoped would be, her surprise question until last.

"Professor Pettermann, I understand you're the main stockholder in a new company called Micropark Enterprises SA? Is that anything to do with your project?"

The professor was taken aback at this, but he shrugged eventually and gave her a warm smile.

"I have no more comments to make now, my dear. Tell that editor, who hired you, to keep things quiet for the moment if he wants an exclusive story. Give me a call in a couple of weeks."

The reporter thanked him and left. Outside the university, she opened her mobile phone and called her editor client. He was disappointed at her news, but confirmed that she should go for the full story, exclusively if possible, and wait until the professor was able to tell her that the project was a success.

A few months later, the newspaper came out with the news that JURASSIC MICRO PARK would be open for business the following holiday weekend. The rest of the newspapers and TV Channels soon picked up the story and, on the opening day, the queues were enormous. Extra railings had to be placed around the access area, to cope with them.

The long impatient wait to get in was well worth it though. The viewing area comprised a large glass walled enclosure containing a miniature jungle with several open pasture areas inside it. Little herds of tiny vegetarian dinosaurs browsed happily, feeding on the clumps of fast growing genetically modified Bonsai trees. There was also a miniature lake in one of the open areas, where the occasional miniature diplodocus could be seen paddling around from time to time, with its long neck mostly up out of the water.

For the benefit of the public, there was a large raised observation gallery all around the enclosure, with closely placed sets of binoculars around it. Viewers were able to see the fantastic creatures in detail. There was also a large transparent roof held up in position over the enclosure. It was suspended from a set of computer controlled apparatus, and could be lowered and effectively sealed if for any reason the environment needed modifying, such as for climate control in the winter.

The whole project was a huge success. Viewing became only possible by purchasing reserved tickets, timed and dated. The money rolled in and the stockholders, and the employees, were delighted; until one day, when unexpected problems began to happen. The first was, when it was realised, that something very hungry was devouring the vegetarian dinosaurs. An unknown predator was at work.

The park manager, Jeff Rogers, first discovered it when routinely scanning around the park area through one of the viewing telescopes. He suddenly saw a heap of tiny bones just visible below one of the larger mini-trees by the side of the lake. Yet at the same time, surprisingly, there seemed to be more of the creatures around than before. A more careful search, with a more powerful short-range telescope, revealed tiny clumps of eggs, with several of them actually in the process of hatching. This was definitely not supposed to happen, as all the original creatures had been cloned in incubators in the professor's laboratory, and they were genetically selected to only be females.

Remarkable too, was the fact that the tiny emerging creatures were clearly not the same species as those already there. Predators were not in the current plan at all. Jeff called the professor urgently, who was soon peering down through the largest tele-microscope. He was amazed at what he saw.

"I can hardly believe it ... but it looks like evolution is at work, they're auto-replicating and apparently mutating too!"

Jeff's wife, Joan, was looking through one of the other instruments, when she suddenly caught sight of a predator, an allosaurus no less. It had been skulking in the jungle, but had just pounced out into a herd of vegetarian dinosaurs. As she watched, astounded, it grabbed and took several bites out of one of them before sneaking back into the jungle again.

"Professor, I think we had better drop the roof over the enclosure. We'll have to seal it permanently. The telescopes and binoculars will have to be bagged into the lower part of it."

The professor agreed and the work began immediately; but meanwhile, the park had to be closed to the public.

The next afternoon, just before the roof was ready, one of the maintenance staff burst into Jeff's office, holding a handkerchief to his bleeding ear.

"You'd better come to the park Jeff. Something new has appeared, and it just bit me."

He removed his handkerchief and partly opened it. Jeff was astonished to see a tiny winged creature, struggling in the folds of the fabric, a pterodactyl no less. He grabbed a specimen jar, and together they managed to deposit the thing safely inside it.

"Where there's one, there must be others." Jeff exclaimed. "We'll have to seal off the entire area. If only the roof had been ready before this happened. Could any more of them have escaped?"

The technician shrugged and shook his head.

"I can't be sure. The self-closing doors should have prevented them escaping from the park itself, but there could be others flying around over the enclosure. This one came at me through the binocular seal I was fixing."

They soon closed off the exit to the park and hastily built a temporary airlock on to the entrance. Later, Jeff donned a self-contained protective suit, then proceeded into the airlock and closed its outer door. He opened the door to the park area, moved out into it and closed the door again as fast as possible. Even so, he just caught a glimpse of something tiny fluttering through the door just as it closed. He called the technician, who was waiting with the professor outside the airlock.

"There's one trapped in the airlock now, I'll try to catch it when I come out. I'm going to look around first."

He went up the steps to the observation platform and began scanning the park area with one of the powerful binocular telescopes. It took some time, but he eventually discovered the remains of a clutch of new eggs by the lake. Examining them carefully using the zoom lens he could see that only two of the eggs could have hatched successfully. The rest were crushed into the ground, with just tiny pieces of creature partly inside them. Clearly something hungry and larger had got to them first. Jeff continued scanning, but found no more predators of any kind anywhere. This was somewhat puzzling. There probably were more, but they must be well hidden. He called to the technician again.

"I'm coming out, everything seems normal. I'll try to catch that other one now."

He opened the entrance lock door, cautiously, but was not quick enough. The tiny furtive creature flashed through the entrance and back into the park area.

Jeff cursed, several times.

"It's gone back into the park area again. We'll have to find it and get it under the roof"

The professor was not worried.

"Leave it there. We'll catch it later. Meanwhile get that roof down as soon as possible."

Once the domed plexiglass roof was in position, the hunt resumed for the missing pterodactyl. Eventually it was located inside a ventilation duct. Jeff captured it with a small vacuum cleaner, the kind used to clean a computer keyboard. Unrolling the squeaking little creature, from the small filter bag, was tricky but he managed it. The professor examined it closely.

“I suspect there are several new species of dinosaurs, in the Park now. They're hiding in the jungle and even when they come out occasionally, they’re too small for us to see them. However, I don't think they are vegetarians. The bones we see now are picked clean and not broken at all, like we get with the larger predators. These new ones must be smaller, maybe a lot smaller."

Time went by and the inevitable mishap occurred. One of the rivets holding the sides of the enclosure together, unknown to the maintenance staff, began to work loose. Eventually it dropped out completely leaving a little hole through which a tiny crafty creature might be able to escape. One of them soon did. Carl Summers, the senior technician burst into Jeff's office one morning.

"Something just bit me, when I was in the park building. Look at my finger, there's a small lump out of it and it hurts. I caught a glimpse at what did it, before I instinctively brushed it away and it escaped. I'm sorry about that because I'm certain it was a raptor, a tiny velociraptor, about a few millimetres high, probably a young one. There must be hole somewhere in the enclosure. We'd better start looking for it!"

The professor joined them and they finally found the rivet hole; low down by one corner, almost hidden by one of the roof support columns. It was clear how the raptor had escaped.

Joan managed to catch another one in the act of escaping. She caught it by one leg with her tweezers. Jeff's magnifying glass revealed it struggling like mad, and trying to bite the metal ends that held it.

"Don't let it go whatever you do." Carl said, apprehensively. "It might ..."

"Oh no!" interrupted Joan, "There's another one about to emerge from the hole. I wonder how many already have?"

Carl stopped chewing and took out his gum. He twisted it into a ball and pushed it hard into the hole.

"That's stopped the little blighter. Get unstuck from that!"

The professor looked up from peering through one of the telescopic viewers again; he became thoughtful.

"We'd better check around and see if any more have escaped. Hallo! There are a lot more eggs in there and I do believe some of them look a lot larger than before. The DNA must be mutating, by itself. I don't think it's safe anymore, to keep the park here. I'm afraid it'll have to stay closed.

Somehow, we'll have to move the whole thing to a more secure place. It's either that or we'll have to destroy the creatures."

Joan was horrified, when Carl, the senior technician had his solution ready.

"Gas them perhaps? Carbon monoxide poisoning might be the easiest way. We could easily connect their air conditioning system to the exhaust pipe of a tractor."

The professor wouldn't even consider the idea.

"I think there's a better solution. Some time back we had an interesting offer, for a complete replica of what we have. A second MicroPark. Maybe that's the answer? I'll call them now and see if we can work something out, with this one."

He returned an hour later with good news.

"I outlined our problem and the probable costs involved in shipping the whole park to their location. They're very interested. I didn't hide anything. They weren't worried about the problems we've had. They're used to creating secure environments for all kinds of creatures."

Jeff and Joan thought it sounded like a good idea, but Carl had to express his doubts.

"Are you really serious sir? The thing is too large to be moved surely, and what about ...?"

Jeff interrupted him, enthusiastically, before the professor could reply.

"No it's not. I've seen larger constructions than that being transported by road, like sections of a bridge for example."
"That's right." exclaimed Joan. "I believe you only have to get permission to use a wide-loading trailer on the route and then arrange for a police escort all the way. It can be done, but where are these interested people; will we have to move the Park very far?"

The professor hesitated and looked a little anxious.

"Well actually, the site they're talking about is in the Canary Islands. There's already a world famous animal and bird park there on Tenerife, the largest island, and now it seems they're building a new one further south. Our MicroPark dinosaurs are just the extra attraction they're looking for apparently. Their offer includes the trip for you three too Jeff, to oversee things. It also includes free accommodation in the nearest five star hotel; and a nice bonus too!"

The trip by road to Portsmouth Harbour was mostly uneventful. The whole MicroPark Unit was delivered safely; and stowed on the deck of a small container ship, a few days later. It had taken longer, for the construction team, to reinforce the walls and corners of the enclosure and make sure that the whole thing would travel safely. Fortunately, having been built on what was effectively a raft constructed from tough sheet aluminium alloy, it wasn't too difficult to put a large wooden frame together to support the complete unit. During the road journey, there were a few braking mishaps, causing some of the herds of tiny creatures to be thrown off their feet. However, they soon got back up again and seemed no worse for the trip.

A week later, when the ship was about half way to their destination, with Jeff and Carl on board to watch over things, a severe storm blew up. The wind screamed wildly and the waves soon built up to deck level. Then, without warning, the freighter was hit by a freak wave. Somewhere two large tankers had created a single, enormous, coincident wave as they crossed over each other. It built up and descended with all its fury on the luckless ship carrying the precious deck cargo.

To Jeff's horror, a vast wall of water came suddenly thundering over the side of the freighter. He was flung to the deck as a stack of containers broke loose, and were swept sideways across the ship. They crashed over and split apart. One of them collided with the crated MicroPark and slid it hard on to the ship's safety rails, at the same time smashing a corner of the enclosure and damaging its roof. Then as the base of the wooden crate shattered against the stanchions, the raft slowly slid over the rails and down into the raging sea. Jeff, Carl and the crew, could do nothing to save it: they were too busy saving themselves.

The MicroPark floated for a while but, inevitably, enough water seeped in to sink it; and the ship's crew could do nothing to save it. It would have been crazy to launch a lifeboat, and they were too busy securing the remaining deck cargo.

Much later, when things had calmed somewhat, Jeff used the ship's radio to report the tragic loss. The professor was still being plagued with the occasional escaped tiny raptor, turning up in the most unexpected place, and having to be dealt with on the spot. He was beginning to think that the only plus left in the whole exercise would be the subsequent insurance claim his company would make, for the destruction of the MicroPark, and hopefully settled with no problems.

The total loss of the MicroPark, and anticipated viewing revenues was demonstrably substantial, although the negotiations were tricky; but after a lot of argument, the professor allowed his company to settle for fifty percent over five years. That was more than enough for the team to think about replacing the Park directly on site in Tenerife, but with many more safeguards built in, to avoid the runaway evolutionary problems previously experienced. The professor paid in the cheque, and his relieved team got down to work again in their laboratory.

Then one fine weather day, but some months before the new park was ready, a Spanish fisherman was pulling in his net off the coast of Andalucia, when he noticed something unusual struggling inside it. Whatever it was soon began to tear into his valuable net with a set of small, but fearsome sharp teeth. He grabbed a boathook and began to beat the creature's head as hard as he could. When it finally stopped moving, he had a good close look at it. He was puzzled at first, but then he remembered. Back home, on evenings when he couldn't be at sea, he'd often watched nature programs on television. He'd even made a recording of one especially fascinating program he'd seen. He was soon speaking fast into his radio microphone and calling the port authorities, back home.

"Yes, it really is. Just like the one, they say they have, up in Loch Ness. I saw a program about it on BBC TV a few weeks ago. It looks just the same to me, as what they said that might be."

The professor was soon informed; he called Jeff and Carl.

"I think it sounds like a plesiosaur. It must have been evolving in our lake, without us ever seeing it. Then it escaped when the first park sank. I wonder what else might have appeared if we hadn't lost it?"

Jeff snorted, and gave him a shrug, looking anguished.

"I wonder what else might have managed to get away? We're still finding escaped raptors, after all this time. We'd better set up routines to check every single egg that appears, even more carefully, with this new park."

The professor wasn't at all concerned.

"Stop worrying Jeff, it won't happen again, now that I've modified the DNA. It will make the replacement business very lucrative, because this time we'll only be cloning males!"

They all grinned, except Carl who added, with a thoughtful look, "But what if they start growing again … possibly even like some of them were originally … up to sixty tons …?

This well publicised process never ceases, of course, and you never know what might appear when you need some help?

EVOLUTION?

Carmen Gonzales lived, with her fisherman husband, in what might be called a comfortable cave dwelling, down in the little harbour of El Puertito, in the lower South Western part of Tenerife. It was built into the rocks, with a large living area and a small cellar, where the fish her husband caught were frozen and stored, before taking it to the restaurants in Los Christianos. Carmen had gone down to the cellar, to tidy up, but she ran into a problem when trying to leave.

It had been an accident waiting to happen, and finally it did. She had become trapped, and had been teasing the cellar door lock with a safety pin for almost ten minutes, but it didn't show any signs of opening. It always looked so easy, when some poor heroic victim had to do it, on the television! It was a moderately windy day, and the ocean surf pounding in the background drowned out any clicks that she thought she was supposed to be hearing. She felt she was beginning to panic.

Then suddenly the door flew open. She fell forward with gasp, and there confronting her, unbelievably ... was a large black seal, very wet and with one flipper resting on the now lowered door handle. Carmen gaped at it in astonishment as it waved the other flipper cheerfully and then began to communicate.

"You … happy now?" Its head was raised and the big brown eyes were looking directly at her, but its lips were not moving. The voice must have been coming from inside her head. She nodded and forced a smile, as the voice came again, softly.

"Me … heard you … call."

Astounded, she realized that must have been well over half an hour ago, when she'd slipped, on the top of the steps, and the cellar door handle had snapped on the inside. Somehow this wonderful, but incredibly impossible, creature had picked up her cry of anguish. It must have understood her plight and, after swimming ashore, had crawled all the way up to the beach house to help her.

"What are … er, I mean, how can I ever thank you? I didn't know we had any seals around Tenerife, except in Loro Parque. Have you escaped?" That was all she could think of to say. The bland expression on the seal's face seemed to change, and she wondered, could it be trying to smile at her?

"No escape ... me passing … happy … help you." It communicated, then the voice paused for a moment. "But … was chasing good fish … hear you call … think all gone now."

The creature regarded her expectantly. Into Carmen's mind suddenly came a picture of her kitchen table and the fat tuna she'd put out to defrost that morning, ready for the evening meal. She knew exactly what to do.

The seal followed her out to the kitchen, its feet slapping, and making a series of wet patches on the newly tiled floor. Carmen picked up the tuna and handed it over. The seal's facial expression seemed to change again as it grasped the fish in both of its flippers. Squatting back on its haunches it began to crunch into the almost defrosted flesh. In just a few minutes the whole fish had vanished. The seal looked around, then bent over and licked up the few, perhaps imaginary, scraps from the floor.

"Good fish …" The voice came, as the seal stretched up and looked straight into her eyes again. "Can be … more?"

Carmen was still feeling very grateful, and after all, there were plenty of the large fish in the big freezer in the cellar. She patted the seal's head and replied. "Just a moment, wait here and I'll get you another one."

The creature regarded her for a few moments, as though listening for something, then nodded slowly. Carmen felt sure it had understood everything she'd said. She went back through the cellar door and descended the steps. She was about to open the big freezer when she heard a sudden sloshing sound and the door slamming shut. She turned and dashed back up the steps in alarm. It was clear to her what must have happened. The over eager seal had followed her and accidently pushed against the door.

"Open the door again, please!" She called firmly, and waited, but there was no answering voice in her head. She tried again, but it was no use, something must have caused the friendly seal to leave and head back into the sea again. Perhaps it was already too far away. She sighed and began to feel around the edge of her apron.

It always did look so easy on the television! Carmen tried teasing the door lock again with another safety pin but it didn't show any signs of opening. The ocean surf was still pounding in the background, drowning out the clicks that she was supposed to be hearing. She began to panic. Her husband wouldn't be home for at least another three hours.

Then the door flew open and she fell forward with gasp of alarm. There before her this time stood, unbelievably ... a very much larger seal, very wet and with one big flipper resting on the door handle. Carmen gaped at it in astonishment, as it spoke, aggressively, inside her head.

"Want fish too … like little sister!"

Carmen reeled back in dismay. There were several other big seals in a queue behind it, and lurching ominously past the kitchen window she was horrified to see something else … a great deal larger.

Tenerife has a history going back a long time, and much of it violent. Certain incidents could well have given rise to various supernatural happenings. How could we get to observe them?

HOLOGHOSTS

My friends and I had arranged to get together for a meal at my local village pub, one fine summer evening. For some reason, our conversation after dinner soon turned to the subject of the, so-called, supernatural. As I reminded them, I´ve always believed that everything apparently still unknown to science, at the present time, will eventually turn out to have a scientific explanation. As to that phenomenon generally known as a ghost, I have always believed, an apparition only needs the right atmospheric conditions to provide the necessary energy for revealing itself. The best conditions seem to be when it's warm and dry, with lots of static electricity in the air; when you get the feeling that a thunderstorm is imminent.

I believe that scenes can be stored in naturally occurring memory chips, the ones created by chance in special kinds of stone. I was convinced that various solid-state components and circuits could have been formed, randomly, in rocks when our planet cooled aeons ago. Certain atmospheric conditions would activate them, to record events taking place nearby. Similar conditions later can reactivate them to reproduce the recorded image. Nowadays, created under modern conditions, we'd call it a hologram.

Jamie, the eldest of my friends, came up with an extremely interesting idea. Perhaps natural memory chips were still being created? What we should do, he proposed, would be to visit a volcano. Perhaps an active one, if possible, and study the rocks it had created in more recent times. We discussed this fascinating idea at length; then another of my friends, Ted, said he knew the ideal place.

He explained that last year he went on a holiday to Tenerife, the largest island in the Canaries, off the North West coast of Africa. He'd taken a coach tour up to the base of Mount Teide, incidentally the highest peak in any part of Spain, and which is apparently still a dormant volcano. All around the flat area at its highly elevated base there are millions of rocks and stones, large and small.

They must have been thrown out from the volcano, and from some of the other craters that had erupted nearby, over the ages and even up to more recent times. There were several areas where he'd seen little rectangular flakes of silica, or some similar material, embedded in the surfaces of some of the rocky lava. They must be spread right throughout it too. He thought there must be millions and millions of them, all formed naturally by the volcano whenever it had erupted. Surely that would be the ideal place to further test the theory?

I was really intrigued, and so were my friends. Some of us were keen on video camera work, so we thought it would be a good idea to make it a film expedition. We decided to visit Tenerife early in March of the very next year. The weather should be good then and the costs in getting there, and staying somewhere locally, were much more reasonable at that time of year. I found out all about the island, using the Internet, and soon realised that it would be best to take some camping gear with us; especially as we wanted to spend enough time up in the area around the volcano to thoroughly investigate things overnight. It turned out to be a very good idea, because there were no hotels close enough to the place, to want to return to, very late at night.

We decided to take a camper van with us. Jamie, my oldest friend has a very good one. It can sleep five easily, and there was also room enough to stow all our equipment. Jamie, Tim, and I drove all the way there with it. It's a long road and sea journey to get to the Canary Islands from England. Apart from the overnight ferry down the Bay of Biscay to Santander, in northern Spain, you then have to drive to Cadiz in Southern Spain and finally take another overnight ferry. That gets you to Santa Cruz, the main port in the North East of Tenerife. Altogether, making it part of our holiday, the trip took us a whole week to get there, but we enjoyed every bit of it. We managed to arrive there before our other two friends, Joe and Fred, and so were able to pick them up from the main airport, in the South East of the island. We also bought several packs of sandwiches from the airport bar to sustain us the following day. Then, after an excellent meal at a small restaurant in a nearby village, we drove on up to a suitable spot to stay the night.

The following morning, we took the camper van further inland and finally up to the base of the volcano. The air was wonderfully clear and the view was spectacular, with snow all around the peak. We parked the camper and then went on foot across the Canadas, as the vast flat area there is called, to a large rock formation known as the Cathedral. Then, farther up above there, we found the outcrops of rock that Fred had told us about. They were truly remarkable. Shiny black and grey boulders were everywhere, with flakes of silica all over their surfaces, and obviously down inside them too. Some of them were like large bubbles of black rock, joined together and emerging from beneath the ground. If any of the flakes were rudimentary chips, and there must be millions of them there, then chance would surely have turned some of them into memory chips; and who knows what else? We could hardly wait to begin our investigations and were eager for it to get dark.

Apart from my video camera, I had brought a special pump-up spray container with me. It had a very fine nozzle and contained a salty, electrolytic, conducting fluid. I hoped to use it to link several chips together. We didn't expect to be lucky enough to experience a thunderstorm, to create the required conditions, so we'd brought a simple high-voltage generator with us instead. A small machine with rotating disks, fitted with insulated segments that slide around against each other. You turn them continuously, with a handle, to generate static charges on them, which build up on a couple of copper ball electrodes. The science department in most senior schools has at least one of these Wimshurst machines, as they're called, and Fred had been able to borrow one. He'd unscrewed the two copper balls and replaced them with some well-insulated cable terminals, so that we could extend the points at which to apply the static voltage.

We were over two thousand metres high, and there was still snow up on the volcano peak, so it got cold very quickly once the sun began to set. However, we were all well protected with the pullovers and anoraks we'd brought with us, so that wasn't a problem. We brewed some tea, ate our sandwiches and then began to try some experiments. I connected the insulated cables to the static generator; then donned my gloves as Fred began to turn the handle slowly. The two cables were fitted with sharp pointed metal rods, and selecting a likely flake on the nearest boulder, I touched one rod to one side of it, and then the other to the opposite side. We had a current meter in the machine's circuit, and it indicated a slight reading. Nothing else happened, so I asked Fred to wind the handle a little faster, which he did.

Suddenly there was a sharp crack and a blue discharge flashed across the surface of the flake. I called to Fred to slow down a little; then I began trying several other flakes to see what would happen. Some of them flashed over at the same settings but some of them didn't and the meter indicated different currents flowing. I felt very pleased; it was already not bad going for a bunch of amateur experimenters. This first test had roughly indicated that some of the flakes might well be semi-conducting.

Meanwhile, Jamie had been experimenting with an electrical resistance meter. He soon reported that several of the flakes appeared to have different internal properties. This was certainly encouraging. Then with a sensitive voltage meter he tried seeing if any of the flakes, I'd treated, had an electrical charge left in them. He soon found one that did, but only one. Joe asked him how many he'd tried. We were all encouraged to hear that this first result was one in thirty-four. This was a very good ratio, even better than we had hoped to discover.

After looking around further we selected a more promising site, a small open space, between several of the large flake covered rocks that almost formed a circle. We set up four camera tripods just outside them and then spread sheets of aluminium foil between each pair; effectively creating two large electrodes, facing each other. We had more than enough heavily insulated cable to connect each of them to the Wimshurst machine.

As soon as we were ready, and it was dark enough, Fred began to wind the handle at a steady speed. Joe stood by to relieve him when he got tired. I walked into the space between the rocks and immediately felt my hair stand on end. When I stood in the middle and stretched out my arms, the hairs on them bent over in opposite directions pointing to the sheet electrodes. I called to Fred to wind a little faster. I was watching the hairs on my right arm as he speeded up the machine. Then I looked up and saw someone coming to join me. However, it wasn't one of my friends. It was a wild looking figure dressed in what looked like animal skins, and carrying a wicked looking wooden club. Our first ghost had already appeared, and all of us could see it very clearly.

Jamie and Tim came over cautiously for a closer look. Fred continued to wind the generator handle at a steady speed, but twisting around slightly to get a better view of the apparition. Joe was still standing by him, staring intently at the strange figure as it approached me. Then it suddenly halted and began to look all around, shading its eyes with the palm of its free hand. I felt an urge to raise an arm in greeting as it finally looked directly at me and then slowly began to smile.

Reason told me of course that, when this scene was recorded, the figure must have seen someone else. I turned sharply and looked behind me, moving sideways at the same time. At first I could see nothing new, then there was a shimmering in the air and a faint second figure appeared. It was a soldier wearing a breastplate and a short skirt with vertical strips of metal around it. On his head was a metal helmet, with a semi-circular disk on the top of it, pointing forwards. His whole appearance reminded me of a picture I'd seen of Spanish soldiers in a museum somewhere, or perhaps in films at the cinema. I glanced around at the others. They were all watching the scene being enacted, including Fred who was somehow managing to keep the handle turning at a steady pace. I looked back again at the two figures, now apparently having a conversation. Their lips were moving, but no sounds came from them. It was clear that we had achieved video mode, but not yet audio! I broke the silence by calling to see if any of my friends could hear anything. Fred replied that he thought he could, coming faintly from one of the rocks close to him. He let go of the generator's handle and pointed. Inevitably, the two figures began to fade as the machine slowed down, and then abruptly vanished. Fred grabbed the handle again and began to wind it furiously. Nothing appeared. He tried several mores times, turning the handle at different steady speeds, but it was no use.

It was beginning to get very cold, and we were all feeling tired. We made a small fire in the open space where the apparitions had appeared and then sat down for a welcome warming drink and a chat about what we'd seen. Ted suggested that the wild looking figure was a Guanche, one of the original natives of the island. The other one was clearly a Spanish soldier. From what he'd read about the history of the Canaries, several detachments of Spaniards had invaded Tenerife many years ago and, after a series of campaigns, had finally conquered the native population. The scene we'd seen might have been one of the natives giving secret information to the enemy, in return for protection, or perhaps he was trying to negotiate peace terms. Maybe our next evening's experiment would reveal something more? Finally, worn out by our exertions and the late hour, one by one we got into our sleeping bags and were soon well asleep.

The next morning, Fred and Joe went back to the camper van and, after a while, they returned with a battery and a small electric motor. They began to rig up a friction drive on the static generator, for turning the small wheel to which the handle was fixed. After an hour or so they had it going smoothly, but only at the one speed. It did seem reasonably close to how fast Fred had been turning it the night before. That had certainly been successful, so we decided to give it a try. It wouldn't be able to run any faster, but we could probably load it up somewhat to run it slower if necessary.

We passed the rest of that day wandering around the area. It was fascinating. There were rocks of all colours and unusual shapes and sizes. We discovered many more likely spots where scenes might have been recorded, and settled on one that was on a slope. There were flake bearing rocks everywhere, but with plenty of space between them for moving about. Unfortunately though, as the evening approached we were frustrated by bad weather. The few clouds that had been around suddenly grew much larger and came lower down. Within minutes we were completely fogged in. Luckily we were very close to the van at the time, so with any more experiments apparently impossible, we decided to remain in it for the night. We enjoyed a good chat, and a substantial hot stew prepared by Fred, then some drinks afterwards, all contributing to a warm and jolly evening.

It was cloudy and cold again the next morning, but later on the weather improved enormously. After a hot lunch in the van we all proceeded over to our amateur research base again, to check out the equipment we'd left there. Fortunately, everything was fine and dry, under the storage covers Fred had thoughtfully provided. We moved everything further up the slope, then sat down and enjoyed some baguettes with dried ham and red wine. After that we began to make the equipment ready for the evening. We unrolled and set up our aluminium sheet electrodes, opposite each other again, on each side of the gradient; but this time we made them even larger and wider than before. Then we were hopefully ready for our next encounter with another ghostly scene from the past. The conditions were perfect and it didn't take very long.

The electric motor made a comforting whirring sound, but we suddenly became aware of something else. Faint shouts and screams, and very faint at first. Then they grew louder and suddenly the space between the electrodes began to be filled with, what looked like, white dust swirling around erratically. Parts of it began to move closer together and coalesce, with other areas clearing between them to reveal the rocks and the slope again. The denser areas seemed to solidify and gradually turn into identifiable shapes, mostly twisting and turning but with some flat out and motionless on the ground.

We soon realised that we were witnessing the edge of a desperate battle. Guanches and invading Spanish soldiers, all hacking away at each other, with swords and other weapons. Some of the natives were wielding rough axes, made from what appeared to be stone wedges bound to stout sticks. Crude, but very effective. There were bodies on the ground everywhere, natives and soldiers, both still and writhing in agony. It was a terrible scene of carnage, and I regret to record that not one of us thought of using our video cameras at the time. I think we were all too shocked at what we saw to react. Joe actually had his camera at the ready, but afterwards he explained that he just froze at the dreadful sight of so much bloodshed. He wasn't the only one.

Then the scene began to flicker and fade in places. The yells and cries were as loud as ever; but it was as if a mist began to form, in patches, which then spread out to fill all the space between the electrode sheets. Finally the mist became uniform everywhere and then gradually faded. We were stunned into silence for several minutes. Fred switched off the generator and spoke first.

"That was unbelievable. I think we should try it again, perhaps further up the slope."

I agreed, and together we moved our equipment to the second location we had selected earlier in the day. There was enough moonlight to see our way, and we had three powerful lamps with us. This time the three of us, who had them, vowed to use our cameras come what may. Little did we know what was to come!

The motor started up again and we waited. We were all on edge after that terrible last scene, but had decided to get even closer to the space between the electrode sheets, with our cameras at the ready this time. Tim set his to run continuously, mounted on a spare tripod. I had even remembered, at last, to spray some of the rocks with my conducting fluid, to try it out. We didn't have very long to wait before the sounds started.

Nothing like last time however, these were dull roars and crashes, and what sounded like muffled explosions. At first, I thought we were going to see another battle, perhaps recorded at a much later date, with cannons being used, but I was very wrong. Suddenly the ground beneath our feet seemed to drop away. Way down beneath us we could see a glowing turbulent sea moving slowly down a slope. We were horrified to find ourselves somehow floating in space, but the space was not empty. Strange shapes began to materialise all around us. They became rocks and stones of all shapes and sizes, whirling around and around and even through us. Our instincts made us try to duck and dodge them. It was a terrifying experience. I saw Jamie, Joe and Fred lose their balance completely and fall over yelling in fear. Ted grabbed me around the waist, then groaned, and slid down, slowly rolling over my feet. Clinging to him, I felt violently sick and could only moan in anguish. Tim was the only one who realised immediately what we were witnessing. He was also nearest to the generator and was able to tear away at the battery terminals and disconnect them. The generator stopped turning and the incredible scene vanished, immediately. Thankfully too, the solid ground appeared back beneath our feet again.

Tim then performed another vital function. He grabbed the whisky bottle, out from our food hamper, and proceeded to pour us all a stiff dose of the reassuring fluid. After that, and somewhat recovered, we sat down to discuss what we'd experienced. Clearly some memory chip bearing rocks must have been already created down inside the volcano at the time of the eruption we'd witnessed. We had experienced a natural, virtual reality, phenomenon; the inside of a three-dimensional recording, of what had taken place way back years ago when the volcano had erupted. It was as if we had been hurled out from the crater along with the rocks and stones, and molten lava. Jamie suggested, with a grin, that the randomly created stone circuits, which had recorded those terrifying scenes, could possibly have been the world's first airborne video camera.

Unfortunately, Tim's digital camera was the only one that had recorded anything permanent for us to take back with us. With the bottle soon empty, we could hardly wait to see it. Tim switched on its replay mode, and then ran the sequence through to view it on the camera's little built-in screen. We gathered around and watched it in silence, at first; then one by one we began to chuckle, and eventually shake with helpless laughter.

Afterwards, we all agreed that the crashing and roaring sounds we heard from it seemed real enough, but the video frames were something else. A truly marvellous, and very comical, series of scenes, of all five of us staggering around and falling over each other. The background was hopelessly hazy, shimmering wildly, and out of focus. It could have been taken on a beach in winter, back in England or almost anywhere similar, in a murky fog.

We sat down for a while on some convenient rocks and discussed what we'd seen, and whether we should try any more experiments. Nobody was very enthusiastic, and we all felt it was time to leave. So we gathered up all our gear, then trudged and giggled all the way back to the camper van, where Jamie soon opened up another bottle. He said it would help us to celebrate the success of our amateur, but seriously scientific, video expedition.

Fred summed it up perfectly, a couple of days later when we were ready to say farewell to the island, with a rueful grin. "Anyone would think we drank all that whisky, before we started our experiments up there. It sure put a whole new slant on the different ways to get stoned."

Here's what we British call a ripping adventure yarn, about an unusual object found in an underwater Tenerife cave.

SALVAGE

I was snorkeling around a small bay on the West coast of Tenerife at the time. That's the largest of the Spanish Canary Islands, off the North West coast of Africa. I've a small apartment near there now, where I stay when I want to get away from it all, especially in the winter. I enjoy exploring and there's plenty of scope for it in Tenerife. Volcanic caves exist everywhere on the island, both on land and even under the sea. The lava flows formed them, rolling over the cooler sections from previous eruptions. Some of those higher up on the land lead into vast caverns filled with fresh water from the snow that melts down from the volcano peaks.

I'd found several small caves off shore, and had dived down where possible to have a closer look. I'm a somewhat cautious person, I have to admit, so I rarely fancy diving down to enter an unknown underwater cave, just wearing flippers and a face mask. Snorkeling is all very well, but once you go under, and the valve in the breathing tube closes … that's it. No more air until you come up again. Catch a leg in a crevice and you have a serious problem. That particular cave was something unusual though. It had a man-shaped entrance, which made me very curious. Coincidence perhaps, but it was just like you always see in those crazy cartoon films, where some unfortunate character crashes through a wall and leaves an impression. I recall thinking perhaps an old time diver, in a suit with a copper helmet, had been forced up against the entrance by some underwater upheaval. The entrance could have been smaller previously and then become deformed when the diver smashed into it. Well, it was a thought anyway, and I was determined to find out if I was right. After all, who or whatever caused it could still be inside the cave. I decided to borrow a set of aqualung equipment and go down there with a friend. Joe, who is an expert diver, was very keen when I told him what I planned to do. He suggested sensibly however, that I get in some proper diving experience first.

A week later, after several practice dives with one of the local diving schools, I felt ready to go. I called Joe and for safety we went on a couple more test runs, before he was satisfied I knew what I was doing. Then after breakfast together, we set off for the spot I'd kept secret until then. An hour or so later we were in the water and diving down to the entrance of the cave. As we neared it I could see that my first idea must be wrong. The entrance was remarkably man-shaped, with clearly defined outstretched arms and legs, but a lot larger than any man living. He'd have to be about nine feet tall! However, at the time I thought it was possible that the entrance had originally been smaller and erosion had made it larger, but still retaining its original shape. There certainly was a strong current flowing through it, and alternately in both directions.

Joe had previously insisted on being first into the cave. I couldn't argue, he had the most diving experience and I was still a beginner. If anything happened to me, he'd be held responsible. I didn't want to think about what I'd do if anything happened to him! It was very dark inside that cave, but the entrance did open out into a much larger chamber. The wall around the entrance was not very thick, so the chamber must have been formed as a large bubble in the lava; as it flowed down into the sea. Then we saw it, the man-shaped object that must have created the entrance, leaning up against the wall at the far end of the chamber. It gave us both quite a shock at first, even though we'd previously speculated, somewhat wildly, about what we might see down there. However, we hadn't prepared ourselves for such an unusual sight as this turned out to be.

It was taller than we had anticipated, easily as much as twelve feet high, with thick tapered legs and arms, and a barrel shaped body. Its feet were sunk in the sand on the floor of the chamber. However, the really weird thing about it was its head. It was very large and sledgehammer shaped. I soon decided that the thing had to be some kind of ancient diving suit, apparently made of metal; and that somebody, or something, could still be inside it. Not much chance of it still being alive, however; it looked like it had been there for a considerable length of time. It was variable in colour, from green to dark brown, and there were several colonies of small shellfish clinging to it, but not much seaweed. There wasn't enough light in there for that kind of growth.

Joe made signs that we should try to move it. We attempted to do that, but it was much too heavy. It was clear that we'd need a boat and some heavy lifting equipment to be able to bring it out of the cave and up on to the shore. We looked around the rest of the chamber, but there was nothing else to see; just debris, scattered around below the entrance, where the object must have originally broken through. Eventually I pointed upwards to indicate that I'd had enough and was ready to leave. Joe nodded in agreement and we swam out through the entrance and soon made our way to the shore.

I was absolutely exhausted. Joe had to help me out of my wetsuit, once he'd got out from his. Then we sat down on the beach and discussed what we'd seen and what to do next. The main thing I couldn't fathom out was the fact that the suit was taller than the height of the cave entrance. Joe had a possible answer. If it wasn't upright when it hit the entrance, say at an angle of about sixty to seventy degrees, it could have broken through the thin lava wall, head foremost. Being very heavy, it wouldn't have swung upright very much, so the entrance shape it made could have been less than its total height. We agreed we'd done enough for our first day's investigation and agreed we should to begin to organize another as soon as possible.

Two days later found us alone off-shore near the cave again in a modest sized fishing boat, hired from a local fisherman. It was fitted with an electric winch on its foredeck and a stout boom attached to its mainmast. The owner used it to fish for lobsters in deep water. We'd rigged the cable from the winch to a strong pulley at the end of the boom. At the working end of the cable we'd attached a small grapnel and were ready to try our luck. We dropped a stern anchor in the calm sea close to the cave entrance. The water was deep enough right over it for us to be able to get a direct pull, but we knew we'd need some distance to avoid snagging our find across the inside of the chamber entrance.

We both went down with the cable and grapnel and were soon inside the chamber again. We'd decided to pull the object out head first, so Joe passed the cable around its broad body, up under the armpits, then secured it to one of the hooks of the grapnel. We then swam back to the entrance, keeping the cable taut behind us. Minutes later we were back, on board the boat, and ready to start running the winch. Checking that everything was secure, I pressed the switch and started the electric motor. The slack was soon wound in and the boat began to move towards the cave entrance. Suddenly the anchor cable took the load and we stopped moving forward. The winch began to groan under the extra strain; then abruptly the cable went slack and I almost overbalanced. Recovering, I braked the cable drum and switched off the electric motor. Joe was over the side almost immediately. I stayed by the winch, ready for anything, staring into the water. I was very relieved when he emerged.

"It's fallen over and is halfway to the entrance! I think it's lost its feet." He exclaimed. "I'm sure it'll come out Okay now as long as we keep the cable straight. The only problem is that we must lift it up somehow over the top of the triangle between the legs-shaped part of the entrance. If the cable slips down, either side, the suit will probably jam its head in the leg space."

"Same problem if we get too near, and the body part gets jammed across the head space." I exclaimed. "Let's give it a try anyway, we might be lucky."

To my surprise we were very lucky. I let go some more anchor chain to get the boat nearer to the cave, then I started up the winch again. The cable wound in smoothly with no protests from the motor. I assumed the enormous suit must have lifted up enough to slide out over the triangular section between the leg spaces, but I was wrong. Joe had gone over the side again and reported that the suit had simply slid along the floor of the chamber and collided with the base of the entrance wall. Its weight and speed, and resulting momentum, was enough to break away the central triangle. The lava wall at that point was too fragile to resist the heavy load we crashed into it. I let the motor run and the cable continued to wind in.

Suddenly Joe raised his head and shouted that we had the suit almost below the boat. I looked over the side and saw the cable was hanging down almost vertically. Then the winch motor began to work harder. Slowly the boat began to heel over alarmingly as the object came beneath the pulley, on the end of the boom, and began to lift upwards. The winch started to groan in protest, and I began to worry about our safety. The boat soon heeled so far over that I had to frantically stop the winch. Any more and the sea would have started to come in over the side and sink us. I looked down into the clear water, and could just make out the weird shaped head of the suit; or whatever it was. I shouted to Joe that I'd have to reverse the winch; the load was too great for our boat. He nodded agreement. Then I found I couldn't reverse the motor, it was one way only. All I could do was release the clutch and let the drum free wheel. This I just managed to accomplish, before the strain became too great.

The cable snaked away and the boat lurched upright so violently that I nearly fell over board. Joe had just managed to grab the side of the boat with both hands, and was plucked virtually up, out of the water, as it righted. I grabbed him and pulled him on board. Together we fell onto the deck in a tangled heap, laughing crazily. We got to our feet and then noticed something very strange. The winch was still whirling out cable, but it wasn't slack. Something was pulling it out. We looked over the side and saw that we'd swung around through one hundred and eighty degrees. The cable was now pointing complete away from the cave and running out very fast. I dashed back to the winch and tried to apply the clutch. It was impossible and we were nearing the end of the cable.

Suddenly the winch drum stopped spinning. The boat lurched forward and the pulley broke away from the boom. The cable soon tightened up again as the boat began to overtake the anchor chain. I recall fearing what would happen. The anchor would break free from the sea bed then be pulled over and dragged a very short distance until it dug into the sand again, or snagged itself against a rock. The chain was very strong, so if the pull on the cable continued, either that would snap, or we'd lose the winch overboard. Fortunately, as it turned out, I was wrong again. We began to move ahead and accelerated so rapidly that the anchor didn't bite. It must have just bounced around, along the sandy bottom. Then we came into deeper water and the anchor and chain just trailed out astern of us. I remember feeling thankful that the winch was in the bow of the boat. If we'd been towed astern at the same speed, the low transom would have been awash and we would have been swamped.

Joe suddenly pointed, in surprise. The cable was lifting higher. What was towing us gradually appeared, rising out of the water. It was our weird diving suit find of course, heading out to sea. We could see that it was planing across the surface at a very steep angle. We both had the same thought, and Joe spoke it aloud. "If that weight goes through anything fragile enough it'll certainly leave an impression, definitely shorter than its actual height."

Our speed increased to the point at which something drastic became essential. I saw an axe on the side of the little wheelhouse and scrambled to get it. Our boat was now veering from side to side, roaring along behind a very impressive bow wave. In a panic, I struck down several times with the axe and finally managed to sever the cable. The boat slowed its mad progress through the water and finally stopped, rocking gently.

Then Joe shouted and pointed ahead of us again. The suit was rising up further, completely out of the water. The cable was still attached to it, snaking around in and out of the spray. As we watched in astonishment, it rose higher and higher and then slowly began to turn in our direction. We were horrified to see it heading straight towards us. Joe got ready to leap overboard, but I was frozen rigid to the deck. Then just before it hurtled overhead, but just missing our mast, it made a fast double roll, winding the cable safely up and around it. We realized then that its arms must really be stubby wings, and its legs were actually a forked dihedral tail-plane. Now we knew why it didn't have any feet. Suddenly its tail dropped and its head pointed upwards. It hung there for a moment, in mid air. Then it accelerated vertically, until it was just a dot in the sky, and finally disappeared.

We never saw it again but we suspected, from the victory rolling display it gave us, that it was grateful to us for rescuing it. The bumps and knocks we gave it must have corrected whatever malfunction had caused it to be stranded in the cave in the first place. As to what it was, we still have no firm idea. It might have been some kind of semi-intelligent missile, possibly lost from a submarine. More unlikely perhaps, but in view of the victory roll we observed, and after a drink or two, I sometimes enjoy thinking it might have been a small space ship, crewed by some very little aliens. Either way, we decided to keep the story to ourselves; who'd believe us anyway, when there were no other witnesses … as far as we know?

You never know what other strange objects might be concealed in Tenerife caves, hidden high up in the mountains ...!

ARTEFACT

Wintering as usual here in Tenerife, I still occasionally go diving with my friend Joe, but lately I've taken to exploring by myself some of the less visited mountainous parts of the island. I've a very good large scale map of the area, a bottle of water and always a couple of sandwiches with me, plus a handy cell-phone in case I run into any problems, which is unlikely. Tenerife is full of caves, and you never know what you might find within them

This episode is about what we found in one of the lava caves high up in the central mountainous part of the island. I won't reveal exactly where, because I want to explore more of the particular area eventually, and hopefully without other people getting to it there first. There wasn't a very large entrance to this particular cave. I made it large enough for me to enter, by breaking off some loose pieces of lava rock around the opening. That wasn't easy. People who have tried will know how tough, and sharp, lava rock can be.

Once inside I looked around, using my flashlight, and discovered
what appeared to be a long tunnel surely leading some way to the interior of that particular mountain. I was well aware that it might be dangerous to explore much further inside the mountain by myself, that's always a mistake when it's a question of venturing into the totally unknown. There was no indication that anyone else had ever been inside that particular cave. I hoped I was the first person ever to find it. Once more I decided to let my resourceful friend Joe in on my latest discovery.

As expected, he was very interested, and a few mornings later found us ready outside the cave, with various useful, but light in weight, items we thought we might need. We entered the cave, and looked around, with our powerful flashlights, and after a while we noticed signs that maybe someone, or something, had been here before us. As we progressed, we could see that the tunnel was almost smooth in places. Protruding parts of the walls and floor must have been removed, presumably to allow easier access. Not by using something crude like a stone though, or even a metal chisel, but by something that had actually melted the lava away. The surface looked like black glass in some places.

The further into the tunnel we got, the smoother it became. Then suddenly it opened out into a large chamber. Part of it was full of water, very clean and cold. I tasted a cupped handful. It was sweet and good, unlike the salty, sulphurous taste of some of the mountain water, from the melted snow that runs down from the slopes of the local big volcano, Mount Teide. The ceiling of the chamber was very high up, and barely illuminated by our flashlight beams. We walked around the small fresh water lake and found another tunnel, directly opposite the first one, leading even further into the mountain.

Checking its walls and roof carefully, we entered it and began to progress along it. Then something struck me, it could hardly be a naturally formed tunnel, it was too straight, and close to circular in section. Straight lines are extremely rare in nature I read somewhere, especially long ones. This tunnel just had to be artificial, but how could it have been formed, and by what or whom?

We continued along the tunnel for some time, until I began to realise that the air was getting warmer. I stopped walking and removed one of my thick gloves. I felt one side of the wall, with the back of my hand, then reached down and touched the floor of the tunnel. There was no doubt about it, the tunnel was now warmer than before. Joe stopped and turned to see what I was doing. Then he too noticed the increased air temperature, and removed a glove to check the wall. We gazed at each other in alarm, as we both had the same idea at the same time. I expressed the scary thought first.

"Surely we aren't getting near to some less dormant part of another volcanic outlet?"

"Not really, that's impossible!" Joe decided, after giving the idea some serious thought. "We're a long way away from where the last eruption took place."

I was not reassured and, I must confess, a little nervous.

"What's that got to do with where the next one is going to be? The last one was as recent as 1909. Geologically speaking, they're quite frequent I'd say; perhaps we're due for another one, any time now?"

Joe chuckled, and gave me a grin.

"Stop worrying Tony! Maybe it is unusually warm here, but it must be due to the residual heat left over from an eruption that took place hundreds, or possibly even thousands, of years ago. Porous lava is a marvellous insulator, and this far inside, some hot spots could retain their heat for a very long time I'm sure."

Then Joe noticed something else, and gulped in alarm.

"What on earth is that?"

As he swung his flashlight around, he'd seen something glinting in the distance, further along the tunnel. Then I saw it too. Something was reflecting the beams from our flashlights. We looked at each other in surprise, then forgetting about the unusual warmth, we shrugged and walked on towards whatever it was. We reached the spot where it was coming from and then had to come to a halt. Something unusual was blocking the tunnel.

Together we gave it as much illumination as possible, and examined it carefully. It appeared to be artificial. We could only see the near side of it, but from the shape of its surface, it looked like it could be a very large ball made of some dull metallic substance, with its surface pitted and blackened. The reflections were emanating from a small aperture in the middle of it, which housed something that looked like a hemispherical mirror. It was a bit dusty, but we could see our distorted reflections in it. I took out a handkerchief and flicked over the surface of the mirror, if that's what it was. The dust came away easily, and our reflections became sharper.

I suddenly had a horrible, wildly fantastic, thought, which made me gulp in alarm.

"Joe, it's dead in the centre of the tunnel. I hope that aperture isn't the barrel of some kind of laser beam weapon."

Joe flinched and gulped too.

"Steady on, it can't be, but I see what you mean. How else could this tunnel have been formed so long and smooth, as well as circular and straight."

"Suppose it gets switched on again, if that is what it is." I exclaimed, nervously hoping I was only joking.

"Not a chance." Joe replied, sounding somewhat overconfident, I thought, when he added." But it definitely is even warmer here. Let´s see if we can move it."

Warily, we put our shoulders against it and had a go at pushing the thing further along the tunnel, with the idea of perhaps seeing past it; and what might be on the other side. Naturally enough though, we couldn´t even budge it, there must have been more of it higher up, out of our view. If it hadn't been for the mirror aperture and the size of the thing, I'd have suspected it was a large, naturally formed, iron bolide, or maybe an enormous one of those spherical balls of rock you see bits of, in souvenir shops, with bluish white crystals inside.

"Forget trying to shift it Joe." I grunted, "Maybe the tunnel stops here, and this thing is solid up against the end wall?"

He nodded thoughtfully.

"You could be right. In that case, the thing must be very old, and have got here before the lava covered it. Perhaps it was using a laser trying to get out?"

"Or maybe it used it to make the tunnel so that it could enter the mountain." I proposed.

"Why would it want to do that?"

"You never know. It might have been escaping from something that was chasing it."

"Like what for example?"

"I don´t know, how could I?"

"I think it´s more likely it landed, or perhaps crashed, here and got covered up by the lava. But perhaps you´re right, but why would it wait so long to try to get away?"

Then I noticed something else.

"Joe, I thought that aperture was in the middle just now?"

We both regarded the giant ball in amazement. It was revolving, silently, which was hard to believe and very alarming.

Very soon, the aperture had moved up, and around, and out of sight; and we were staring at the, very grubby looking, base of a large metallic sphere. I glanced down, and could just see a lighter coloured ring all around it. It looked like it was made of some kind of ceramic material. I shouted to Joe.

"Let´s get out of here, fast; I think that's a rocket motor underneath it!"

Joe didn´t argue, even if he thought I was crazy. We dashed back along the tunnel and had just stumbled into the larger chamber, with the small lake, when there came a violent thundering roar. A blast of hot air came hurtling along the tunnel, towards us. We couldn´t see it, but we could certainly feel it. Joe dived into the water and I fell in after him, with my eyelids tightly closed. A few moments later, I opened them again and saw an orange red glow shining above the surface of the water. I struck out and swam deeper to the far side of the lake. The glow faded and, gasping for breath, I ventured my head up partly out of the water. Joe was ahead of me.

We looked back along the tunnel, but the sphere had vanished. All around where it had been, the rock was glowing. Scared stiff, but elated at our escape, I shouted to Joe.

"Now we know what this tunnel side was for., a vent for its rocket exhaust gases. Without this chamber and the lake in it we´d have been roasted."

We dragged ourselves out of the water, and staggered back along the tunnel to the entrance. Once outside, we looked up into the sky but could see nothing. Clearly, further up the mountain there should be a large hole now. If anything had been covering it, it would now be exposed. However, we were in no condition to go up and look. Instead, we made it back down and later were very glad to be back home, still in one piece.

A couple of mornings later, we did make it to the top of that particular small mountain. Unfortunately, there was nothing very interesting to see. The small peak was flattened slightly though, because all the loose rock up there had collapsed into the hole, and filled it, or so it seemed to us; and the ground around there certainly still felt slightly warm. When we went back down to the entrance of the side tunnel, and ventured into it again, we found we could only get as far as the chamber with the lake. The tunnel on the other side had caved in too, so that was the end of that adventure.

From time to time, we cautiously enquired around the various local bars and cafes but, just like that underwater salvage operation last time, nobody had noticed anything unusual, as far as we know; especially something as strange as a large black spherical object, with a glowing exhaust trail underneath it, shooting up into the sky.

Strange objects discovered in Tenerife might not only be weird machines, what about something alive, and objectionable?

BAGGAGE INCLUDED

The breeze was chilly now and the faint distant thunder promised an early winter storm. Maria shivered and walked faster, aware of the muffled muttering coming from the roughly woven sack she was carrying in her arms.

"Quiet you obnoxious little beast!" She snapped, "Or I'll drop you in the barranca*, before we get there."

She had found it, sleeping in her woodshed, that afternoon. She had no idea what or who it was, but she definitely didn't like the look of it. Small, squat and very ugly, covered in sticky black hair, even its mother wouldn't have wanted to know it. She had leant against the wall of the shed, regarding the thing for some time but, ready to run if necessary. It was hideous, and she didn't like the horrible snoring noise it was making. Then suddenly, it woke up, rubbed its eyes and spoke to her in a grating grumbling voice.

"What sector is this then?" It enquired, in a hostile tone. "Where is the nearest terminal?"

Maria was amazed. "You - you can speak Spanish?"

"What else? That's what you use here, isn't it?"

"Well yes, but you don't look like you could know Spanish, let alone speak it."

The weird creature snorted in annoyance.

"How would you know what an expert linguist like me looks like?"

She had no answer to that, so she changed the subject.

"What do you want then? What do you expect me to do for you?"

"Like I asked you." it snapped. "Where is the nearest terminal?"

"What kind of terminal do you mean?"

"One where I can move on to somewhere else of course."

"Well, there's a bus stop at the end of the road leading into the village."

"What's a bus then, and why does it stop? I want a conveyance that keeps going, on to the next terminal."

"Look here!" She cried in exasperation. "I've no idea what you're talking about, but if you want to get to somewhere else fast, then that's the nearest place if you're walking."

"Walking? I never walk. I use instantaneous transportation everywhere I go. I don't walk; it's not what I do. How far away is it back to that terminal?

"About half a kilometre, that's all."

"Impossible! I'll never make it, No wonder I'm totally exhausted. You'll have to carry me back there, if there's no other way. No bouncing me around either."

"So how did you get here in my shed?"

"It was getting dark when I arrived, and I couldn't find the buttons. I saw a light in your habitat and I had to crawl all this way to find someone to help me."

Maria had a kindly nature, and began to feel sorry for her weird visitor.

It took some time to coax the creature into the sack, but she finally made it and set off for the bus stop. Despite the occasional outburst, they eventually arrived there with plenty of time to spare. She opened the sack and whispered in to it.

"The next bus comes in twenty minutes." She explained. "It goes into Los Christianos. From there you can take another one to almost anywhere on the island, to the airport if you want. How much money do you have on you?"

"Money, what's money? Why do I need it?"

She could see this was going to be difficult.

"Where do you think you are, on another planet? You need money here to pay to travel anywhere … to buy things to eat and drink. You have to have it here, to be able to do anything."

“Nonsense, I don’t need it, I’m a privileged traveller, with a special baggage permit."

She shrugged, and thought, “I'll give it enough coins to get into town. Why not … anything to get rid of this pest?” Then aloud she said.

"If I let you out now, will you behave?"

"Of course I will, I only want to get away from this unfriendly place, wherever it is."

Maria gingerly undid the bag and rolled back its opening. The creature slid out on to the seat in the bus shelter and regarded her.

"There must be a terminal request button somewhere in here." It stated confidently. "You'll have to help me find it."

The bus shelter was built against a large rock. A poster on it showed the expected times of the bus, and to where it would be going. She regarded it carefully.

"I see nothing about any special terminals." She exclaimed.

"Look all over the rock at the back."

Maria climbed up on the seat and carefully scanned across the rock, moving steadily from side to side, and feeling somewhat foolish. The creature watched her.

She paused, suddenly.

"Could this be what you wanted?" She enquired. There were two strange looking bumps illuminated on a smooth part of the wall. Each of them had a circular crack around it, which was clearly unusual.

"Yes, if you have found them, those are the call buttons, to take you in either direction. Press the right hand one and I'll soon be away from here."

Maria felt relieved. She pressed the right hand button hard and immediately a pale white beam of light shone down from somewhere above the translucent roof of the shelter. It illuminated them both.

"That's it, that's it!" screamed the elated creature. "I knew it must be here. Now all I have to do is activate this terminal."

The creature pulled out a small pack from somewhere inside its furry body, and pressed one of the buttons on it. Maria moved out of the light rapidly, she certainly didn't want to go anywhere else, but she was curious to see what might happen.

Several minutes passed, and the creature started to become restless. Maria knew the regular bus was due to arrive shortly, but then what? She yawned, and had just decided to leave the creature alone, to get on with it, when suddenly, the beam of light expanded and filled the whole road; just as the next TITSA bus approached and stopped, directly beneath it. There came a deafening crash and the familiar landscape vanished.

Maria blinked in astonishment and looked around. It was broad daylight and she was standing, with the creature, in what looked like the middle of a small village. The front half of the local bus was in the road, right next to them; but with its back end resting on the ground. However, it was not the village she knew. Nobody was about, the little houses were all different; and some of them seemed to be on legs. She scratched her forehead in surprise, the creature seemed puzzled too.

"This is not my terminal." It grated. "But I'm sure you pressed the right button. There must be a malfunction, what are you going to do about it?"

Maria had had more than enough. "Nothing!" she cried angrily, "I should have thrown the bag, and you, into the barranca. You and your precious special permit, what can I do about it? I want to go home too." Unfortunately, there didn't seem much point in trying to walk back. In daylight, from the bus stop, she should have been able to see her familiar cottage in the distance. But she couldn't, everything was very different.

There were only two people on the half bus, in separate seats; plus the driver who was a large local villager named Pedro. The engine, being at the missing rear of the bus, had presumably stopped; so with nothing else to do, he got out. His passengers stayed where they were. One of them was gazing open-mouthed at the scenery, the other one was asleep despite the jolt he must have experienced. The driver looked around and then began to jump up and down in frustration.

"Where are we, what on earth has happened, how come it's suddenly day-time?" Then he saw the creature, and recoiled in disgust. "What on earth is that thing?" He demanded.

The creature gave him a pitying look. "Earth it isn't, stupid." it stated. "Look at the sky."

Maria and the driver looked up together. The sun was there, even though it looked a different colour, perhaps a little more reddish. But there were two bright moons in the sky, almost overhead, and one of them was larger than the other.

Pedro went pale. Maria gulped and began to look around for another pair of terminal buttons. Then she realised the last thing she wanted was to go on further to somewhere else and the creature had the gadget that activated the process. She grabbed the creature firmly again, and then called the driver.

"We have to cross the road and take the next one back!" She exclaimed. "Please help me hold this thing and then find the correct button."

Pedro was too bewildered to argue. He got out of the bus, and allowed himself to be led across the road with the creature, which was protesting angrily, to a small shelter. It looked promising, especially as there was a panel on its wall, with a row of big buttons. She gazed at it in frustration, having no idea which one to press. There was a small sign over each button, but written in no language she could understand. She turned to the creature and asked for an explanation.

"This terminal is not for where I want to be, but it is one of those places from where you can be taken in any direction." It muttered. "Unlike that last dump, where you got on with me."

It pointed to one of the buttons gleefully. "That's it ... there's where I live." It reached up and was about to press the button, when Maria grabbed and pulled its arm away.

"Which button will take me back to my stop again?" She demanded.

"Why should I tell you, you haven't been very helpful to me have you?"

Maria gripped the little creature more firmly with one hand and reached for the sack, which she'd fortunately tucked into the belt of her overcoat.

"Tell me immediately or in you go again."

"It's that one in the middle." Came the outraged reply, followed by a screech of protest.

Pedro, the bus driver, was not impressed. "What about me and my bus … and those two passengers?" He wanted to know. Maria thought about the situation.

"We'll all get back in after this creature activates its control unit." She replied, hoping she'd be able to trust it, otherwise there seemed to be no other choice. Then she heard it give a snort and saw its upper lip curling. She decided it couldn't be trusted.

"You'll come with us, or else!" She grated. "Then you can carry on home, by yourself, from our bus stop again."

The creature screeched in protest, again, even louder. Maria wanted to put it back in the sack, but soon realised that it wouldn't help things, if it was then unable to activate its control unit.

After a lot of aggravation, the creature reached up and pressed the middle button. Nothing seemed to happen.

"You haven't activated your control pack." Gritted Maria.

"I know. We all have to get back into that ancient transport first." The creature insisted.

The driver crossed the road and climbed up into what was left of his bus. He sat down on the first ordinary seat near the front, as there didn't seem to be much point in taking the driving seat. Maria, firmly holding the creature, joined him. The passenger, who had got out, followed her; taking the next seat. The other passenger was still asleep.

The creature took out its control pack and pressed a button. The alien scene vanished, only to be replaced by another, just as strange. They were alone in the middle of a vast sandy desert. There was no wind, it was very hot; and nothing, and nobody, was in sight. At that moment, the other passenger woke up and gazed around in astonishment. He clutched the back of his seat in alarm, when he saw the alien.

The creature wailed. "This place is not what we want either." Then it added brightly. "But I do recognise it. See the two suns, it's an eclipse!"

Maria managed to avoid looking at them; instead, she grabbed the control pack and pulled it away from the creature. The other three humans were gazing out in terror at a large red sun that almost filled the sky, and a smaller bright white one superimposed over it. With the loss of its control pack, the creature started wailing again, a nasty nerve-wracking wail.

"I promise, I will get it right this time. There's a terminal box just behind us, I've been here before. Please don't damage my controller, I'll never get back home without it .... but neither will you! "

Maria and the driver, with the creature behind them, got out of the bus and walked around it. Sure enough, just behind the gaping open end of the bus, there was a small pillar. There was a row of buttons built into its top.

"This is your last chance." Maria stated.. "Pick the right button this time, or back in the sack you go, with no controller, and be dumped here … forever!" She wasn't at all sure about that threat, but it seemed to work. After all, she could try all the combinations of buttons pushing by herself if necessary. Sooner or later, hopefully she'd hit the right one … however long it took.

The creature seemed to be terrified. It examined the buttons and the strange writing above them very carefully. Then it turned to Maria with a simple question.

"Is your home place on Earth called Tenerife?" Maria was overjoyed.

"Yes it is ..!" She exclaimed. "Come on. Let's go … just press the stupid button … now!"

The creature did just that, very carefully, and grumbled. "Now we must all get back inside the bus ..!"

Once inside, Maria held the control pack tightly away from the creature and asked which button to press.

"That one in the middle." Came the muttered reply.

Maria still didn't trust the creature. "Are you really sure about that?" She queried. "Honestly?"

"Yes, definitely, I promise. Please don't leave me here."

Maria sighed; she closed her eyes, crossed her fingers and pressed the button. There sounded the now familiar crunching and grinding noise.

To her, and the other humans', relief they were back at their own bus stop again. However, their half of the bus was now in the road, facing the other way, on the opposite side of the other half. The driver shrugged with relief and became philosophical.

"Even if we'd been returned on the other side," he said, with a glum expression," the two halves could never have joined up properly."

The creature peered up at Maria, timidly. "Can I go home now please?"

"I'd be glad if you would. Do you know which button to press?"

"I think so, but you must give me my controller back first."

"No way ..!" Maria thought. "Not until we're well out of range of that beam it activates."

They all climbed out of the half bus, with the creature still held firmly between Maria and the driver. They went into the shelter and Maria pointed up to the two buttons.

"I think I should press the left hand one this time … right?"

The creature nodded, several times.

Assured, Maria reached up and pressed the button.

"Right!" She shouted to the others. "Now let's get as far away from this shelter as possible."

She sat the creature on the seat of the shelter and let it go. Likewise the driver; then they all turned and ran, but not before Maria placed the controller at the other end of the seat. The creature shuffled along sideways and grabbed it. Then it reached up, on its spindly legs, and pressed the left hand button.

The humans stopped running when Maria said it would be safe. Then they turned and watched. Suddenly, it still being dark, the wide beam came on and illuminated the whole road again. There was a flash and a grinding noise. The creature vanished, along with the front half of the bus.

Maria led the weary travellers along past the barranca, to her little villa. There, she planned to make some coffee and telephone the local taxi for them. All the way there, the driver was muttering to himself. Then he caught Maria's arm.

"They'll never believe me back at the depot, when they recover just the back end of my lovely new bus … I've only had it a week!"

Maria grinned. "And I keep wondering, if that creature's baggage permit included anything as large as the front end of a brand new TITSA bus?"

** A barranca is a ravine, formed in between two lava flows.*

Now for something different, a sample of one of my other activities, which I performed on stage once, in another island; as a supporting act to Roger McGough, one of the celebrated Liverpool poets ...

INSIDE INFORMATION

I went to the Loro Parque* today
to gen up those gawky gorillas
They'd said they were sorry for humans
for the way we're all caged in
I tried to explain that THEY were
but their minds were all made up

Their world was outside a big cage
which kept them safe from us
They had no doubts at all
they'd been around it often
I considered their point of view
What if their cage was larger?
and bordered by the Equator?
Those gorillas are lateral thinkers

Now I'm considering my skin
which I used to believe was around me
with everything loose kept inside
But looking at things this other way
my skin goes around the universe
so my insides could be outsides
The thought, of it makes me uneasy
I don´t really like the idea
of apes and fleas and people
scratching around inside ME!

** Loro Parque is the world famous Bird, Fish and Animal Park here in Tenerife.*

Yes, I've done some inventing in my time, but not in Tenerife ...as yet. However, it would be a good place to try out something really novel ... and intended to be utilised locally.

HILLYBOOTS

Hans Weiser hated walking uphill; it always made him breathless. Now that he was retired, the older he got the more difficult it became. Downhill was no problem. Neither was flat and level, just uphill. He had been a Design Engineer with the Adolf Klomp Company, in Vienna, which specialises in the development of computerised gadgets of all kinds. He had been one of the design team that had produced the first prototype of the Klomp Automatic Teeth*, now much improved, in full production and selling well.

He decided to do something about his problem. He fitted telescopic soles to his strongest walking boots. Fully extended they acted a bit like short stilts, but only about four normal steps high. All he had to do was extend them fully at the bottom of any steep bit of path, then step forward. They were each fitted with a tiny camera and a powerful stepping motor. As each foot moved forward it would scan and calculate the next height and distance then reduce the telescopic part of the boot to ensure that the step forward stayed on the initial level. Thus by moving forward steadily, the boot always stayed level until the telescopic section was fully closed. Then by fully extending them again he'd be lifted up to the next level ready to proceed forward again, and repeat the procedure.

Hans had to strengthen things somewhat and boost up the motors a bit, but after a while it all worked fine. He was delighted to discover that it would even go up steps as well. He realised that if he could make the telescopic sections go even higher, he'd surely speed things up, but he suspected that to be higher up initially could be unstable and shaky. The prototype worked beautifully on slopes that weren't very steep, but on very steep ones he'd only be able to manage one effective level step at a time. In effect his invention was like having a movable, flexible triangular, block under his feet; in other words, a reversed inclined plane, but with a lift to shove you up on top of the front part of it. You'd just walk forward normally to its end, then stop and have it moved forward. Then you'd go up it again. Like turning slopes into long steps, but with something to lift you up on to them each time.

One evening, he saw a video advert for those new rolling platform gadgets, you just stand on and lean to go forwards. They always balanced the rider, and could even go up slopes if they were not very steep or slippery. No way they could they go up steps though, but his invention could! Hans could even go upstairs at home with his mobile gadget. The chairlift he'd been contemplating was now not required, and he'd save money. If that expensive rolling gadget was selling now, then so would his invention when it was ready to be marketed. Thanks to his disability, he´d never got around to going off on a vacation since he was retired. Now things were different, he always wanted to go to the Spanish Canary Islands, so now was his chance. He looked them up on the Internet and soon found some tempting offers.

A few weeks later found Hans happily located in a nice room in the Hotel Los Gigantes, situated in the South West of the island of Tenerife. He couldn´t speak any Spanish, but his English was good. He chose the place deliberately because it was virtually a British colony, but with some German residents, and definitely very hilly. There was one wicked hill, leading up out of Los Gigantes, that the British residents knew as Cardiac Hill. It was the perfect site to test his new invention, before seeing if his old company would be interested in marketing it.

He left the hotel and walked around the area, but in his normal shoes, then decided on a familiar looking restaurant in which to spend the evening. He became very friendly with the one of the waiters who knew some German, had a long chat, with more than a few generous drinks, and finally staggered back to his hotel.

The following morning he was up early wearing his HillyLift Boots, as he´d thought of calling them. He walked along to the foot of Cardiac Hill and then switched them on.

The sidewalk up the hill was horribly steep initially, then reducing to just very steep thereafter. It was the perfect place to try the boots out and he soon discovered that they were even more successful than he´d hoped. He took things slowly at first, but once past the short extremely steep first part of the hill he let the boots speed up. The parallel connected micro-pumps, inside each boot, had to push the hydraulic fluid out from the reservoir, located in the sole, and up into the pistons which operated the multi-telescopic legs. There was a limiting speed for this, but it was acceptable. Half way up the long twisting hill he knew he had a success on his hands, and he could see ways to improve his balance when moving forward. The servo-sensors in each boot reacted faster if he kept his arms outstretched. It would be simply a matter of careful instructions in the handbook and demonstration videos, he was already considering.

He spent the rest of his stay enjoying himself, especially eating out, in what had now become his favourite restaurant.

The day after his return home to Vienna, his old chief, Alfred Klomp, was pleased to see him and soon became interested in Hans´ invention. He got the relevant teams together and together they worked out a production and marketing plan. Even Walter Gotch, the fussy chief accountant expressed his approval. He was due to retire the next year himself, and had already found he had to puff somewhat, when walking uphill. The estimated retail price for the boots worried him though. He told the marketing chief it would probably need to be, at least, around three hundred and fifty euros a pair. He was relieved when that amount didn´t seem to worry anyone else. The marketing chief even thought they could probably go as high as four fifty. The boots looked like a hot product to him, especially as some parts of the world were becoming full of wealthy company pensioners.

Six months later and they were ready. However, three days before the full-scale product launch, a large foreign looking envelope arrived on Alfred Klomp´s desk. He opened it and found inside a comprehensive sales leaflet announcing a wonderful new product, now being manufactured in China. White-faced he called in Hans and the marketing chief and let them read it. It was written in, a somewhat fractured version of, English and illustrated a mass produced copy of their new product. What hit them the hardest, was the recommended European retail price stamped on the back of the leaflet; just ninety-nine euros and ninety-nine cents a pair.

"Walter will go through the roof!" Alfred Klomp muttered. "That´s less than the cost of all our components. Somebody go and fetch him."

A few hours later, when the Accounts Department chief had finally cooled down, they had to reluctantly agree to drop the project. The first production run though, which was ready, would be retained as a retirement option for the staff members, when their time came. Poor Hans acknowledged everyone's sincere regrets on his behalf and drove back home, horribly disappointed. He picked up his mail and discovered a similar large, Chinese stamped, envelope in with it. He threw it across the room in disgust, but later after a long strong vodka, he decided to open it. Inside, in addition to the same leaflet, he found several large photos and a short letter.

The photos showed someone walking, or rather moving, up a very steep hill. There were a couple of palm trees in the background of one of them. Hans recognised Cardiac Hill in Los Gigantes, Tenerife, as well as himself and the special boots the figure was wearing. He unfolded the letter, and read ….

Honoured sir, Mr. Hans

We have noticed that you are named, in a recently published Patent, as the first inventor of these boots. Therefore, we have reserved part of the price for each sale to be sent to your account, wherever you choose this to be. Depending upon the demand, this will be the non-negotiable maximum amount as appended below.

Humbly yours

§%$&")&(%$(/§$

The signature was in oriental characters, but the numbers and words below it clearly read *"00.50 (nought nought. five nought) euros."*

"Oh well, it could be worse," Hans thought ruefully. "I suppose it must have been that first waiter I met. There really are a lot of Chinese restaurants on Tenerife."

* *This refers to the tall tale entitled* ***TEETHING TROUBLE****, which appears in my first collection* ***FUTURE REASSURED****.*

This cautionary tale is about someone foreign, planning to reside somewhere else, in a much warmer place ...and, I can recommend a good one. Incidentally, computers haven't been with us for very long yet, but already we couldn't manage our lives, or moves, without them, could we?

RETIREMENT PLAN

Harald Reiner was a neat and tidy, methodical man. Unattached, since his wife divorced him, he had finally become a pensioner; but deliberately delayed. He had not really enjoyed his job in the bank in Vienna but his plan, in staying on longer, was to ensure that his subsequent, and well-deserved, total remuneration would be increased. His budget calculations indicated that he would thereby have a useful sum left over, each month, from his daily needs. He had enough saved too, to cover any unforeseen emergencies, and wanted to use his pension surplus to see something of the world. He knew that this ambition wouldn't exactly come cheap, even sampling whatever last minute offers he could find. Finally ready now to investigate, he went into town one day and explored what was on offer, from the various travel agents and other places. He was soon disappointed to discover that most of what was on offer was not very exciting and definitely expensive.

Then in his regular bar one morning, someone told him that the best way to find cheap vacation offers was to look them up on the Internet. He decided to follow that piece of advice and, the next day, he drove into town and wandered into the nearest Internet Cafe. He was reassured to see some other older people there occasionally clicking their mice; as well as a couple of teenagers, with their eyes locked to their screens and frantically tapping away at their keyboards. There was someone, apparently in charge, at the end of the row of machine booths, but nobody seemed to be watching what he was doing there, so he sat down at one of the terminals. He gazed for a while at the screen, then down at the keyboard. Surprised at his courage, he tapped a few of the keys experimentally. Immediately the screen went blank. He stared at it for a few moments, mentally getting ready to leave, then he noticed that a slightly older teenager had appeared and was watching him, as well as another older client, nearby; and occasionally sighing and glancing up at the ceiling. Harald beckoned him over. It was the person he'd noticed, at the end of the row, wearing a long green coat; signifying authority and experience.

After about an hour's personal instruction, Harald was able to locate and display a gloomy local weather forecast, and a long series of fascinating foreign football results, all by himself. Feeling exhausted he decided that was enough, for a successful first attempt, and went home to think. Then later he added a new item to his budget to cover the cost of regular visits to town and the cafe.

He visited the place several times over the next couple of weeks and somewhat reluctantly, with the assistance of the supervisor, usually a different teenager each time, he eventually located the Last Minute Travel Offers web-site for his area. He was very impressed at the size of it. However, there was nothing being offered that really fitted in with his current situation; because it was already getting dark, and the only offer that did interest him was leaving the next day, early in the morning, and he wasn't even packed.

Later back home he went over his budget very carefully. To take full advantage of what he had learned, he decided he needed a computer of his own. It was a long way into town, to the cafe, and the weather was so unpredictable. He checked his savings account and, the next morning, drew out an adequate amount to cover his intended purchase.

A few days later, with his suitcase was packed, a friendly driver arrived with a brand new computer, in a very large box. It was a special, free delivery, offer from the local supermarket.

The man helped him get it into the house and then rapidly wished him good luck.

It took Harald a week to set it all up and get it working. He couldn't understand the handbook until something he tried finally did work, then it began to make some sense. After few more patient, but frustrating, hours later he at last managed to log on to his local service provider. Eventually, his screen display looked the same as the one in the Internet Café. Highly elated, he hit the right combination of key presses and mouse clicks and found the weather forecast again. He was overjoyed to be at last on the right track, so taking a deep breath he entered the address of the last minute holiday offers to see what was going.

The very first offer, on the long list this time, was very interesting. Leaving in two day's time was a remarkably low priced trip to Tenerife for a week, to stay in a very nice hotel in Puerto de la Cruz, a place he'd often read about and would love to visit. He sat gloating at the screen for a while, looking at the pictures of the hotel and its surroundings, and then decided to go ahead. Maybe he´d like it enough to want to sell up and move there for good.

When he had the cursor in the right place on the screen, he clicked the left hand button on his mouse. Form after form appeared, which he carefully filled in, more than once. Finally, after several attempts he had his Debit Card number accepted. Up on the screen then appeared a message stating that his ticket would be sent to him, as an E-Mail, right away. All he had to do was print it out and present it to the check-in desk at the airport. Unfortunately, he hadn't done anything about setting up an E-Mail facility. He was about to drop everything, when a message suddenly appeared, in the middle of the screen, requesting him to telephone the travel company's office as soon as possible. He logged off the site and the server and switched off the computer. He still felt close to dropping the whole idea, but they'd already got his money. He felt, for certain, that it would be quite a hassle to get it back, if he ever could.

Finally, he picked up the telephone and dialled the number, which he had carefully copied off the screen and down into his notebook. It took many expensive minutes to fix everything, after he'd got past all the automatic questions and number key pressing requirements, all the various voices requested. However, the very last one was a real live human operator who helped him to decide what name his E-Mail address would be. She told him he'd essentially need a security code for it, but the service provider would prompt him for that. Finally she informed him that his reservation was definitely now secure, and if he went back on line, his reference number and ticket would be there waiting for him.

Reassured, he sat down at the computer and switched it on again. Then he opened the handbook and read the section explaining how to set up E-Mail addresses, as many as ten different ones if he wanted them. He decided just the one would be enough and began to go through all the procedures. After only a couple of hours, he was at last the proud owner of his very own personal E-Mail address. Mentally crossing his fingers, he clicked on the part of the screen now telling him that an E-Mail message was waiting for him. Actually, there were several, when he clicked and displayed the next screen. The first was welcoming him as a new subscriber. The second, third and fourth, were invitations to buy products and services he didn't need. The fifth sounded more interesting but dubious, and that was all. Nothing from the travel company, but he decided maybe it was only delayed and would appear later. He decided to be patient and wait.

With nothing else to do, and not being interested in trying out any games, for the first time he began to look carefully at all the various lists and announcements still on the screen. The handbook explained that he was looking at his server's home page, showing all the interesting and useful things it provided for him to enjoy. He read each of them carefully, one after the other, but was not impressed. Then he saw one that asked if he'd like to check his life expectancy. He wasn't sure if he really wanted to know about that, but suddenly realised that it could be useful. He could check the years left to him and compare the quantity with his pension surplus, his budget and his savings, and see how many places he could really afford to visit. He'd really enjoy making all the plans. The more he thought about it, the more he liked the idea. Perhaps he could afford to stay in Tenerife for two weeks, or perhaps even longer? He could hire a car, and travel around to really see the place.

He moved his mouse and clicked the reply box on the screen, below the announcement. There was a short pause, then up came a long questionnaire. He could see how long it was by the length of the moving arrow space on the right hand side of his screen. There were many personal questions. The first one wanted his age, the second his height, and the third his weight. After that, it was all about his health and that of his parents. Next, it wanted to know about his habits. He decided to be honest, and why not? He felt fine and always enjoyed his cigarettes, and his beer in the local bar, as well as the occasional vodka, and there was no reason why he shouldn't continue to do so. The whole idea of a happy retirement was surely to enjoy it, for as long as possible, while it lasted. He added up and worked out the points, these habitual comforts represented, and entered the details of them where indicated.

Finally he was done. The program then asked him to scroll through the screen and check to see if he'd missed out anything vital. Harald did this very carefully, making only a couple of minor changes, then he clicked the '***Finish***' box and waited. Suddenly the screen cleared and the result of his analysis appeared in a big box, in the middle of it, in large flashing red numerals. He gazed at it in surprise at first, then consternation, followed by horror. There had to be some mistake, because it showed the number ***seventy***. He glanced at the time and was horrified to see that it was only a few minutes to midnight, and tomorrow was his birthday, the seventy-first. He shook his head in disbelief and dismay, then gave a horrible groan, as he shuddered and clutched his chest.

The last thing he noticed, before everything went black, was the E-Mail box at the top of the screen flashing the arrival of a new message.

... and the moral to this tale? Never leave things too late!

This little episode was inspired by a minor incident that happened, in England, some time ago now; but the way technology is progressing nowadays, the following extrapolated situation might well occur almost anywhere, in the not so distant future.

INFORMAL CONVERSATION

"Darling, would you please help me with this form I have to fill in? It's really too difficult for me."

"Sure sweetheart, what is it about?"

"Well, it was kind of you not to mention it but, you know that little accident I had with my car last week, when I went shopping? You know, to that new Mercadona supermarket up the hill."

"Yes, I did notice the damage to the near-side lights, but it didn't look too serious, and I didn't want to embarrass you. I guess nobody was hurt, otherwise you'd have told me about it before."

"Yes of course dear, but I've just had the estimate from our garage to get it fixed, and it does seem a bit expensive. They suggested I make an insurance claim to cover the cost. I think this is the form I need. I found it with the documents in the car."

"Okay sweetheart, so what's the problem?"

"It's these questions about how fast I was going, at the time of the accident, and how fast did I think the other vehicle was going."

"Sounds simple enough, what's the problem?"

"Well, my car was stopped at the time, but ....."

"So, put down zero mph for yourself and what ever speed you think the other vehicle was doing before it hit you. I don't think you'll have any problems with the claim."

"Thank you for your help dear, but I don't know what speed the other vehicle was doing. How could I tell when I couldn't see it clearly at the time? It was moving away from me too."

"What? Just a minute, I don’t understand. Was it dark or something? Didn't you see its lights?"

"No, but yes … at the time it was dark, and it definitely didn't have any lights."

"Well, that's another good point in your favour, but we'll have to have a guess at its speed. From the damage, I'd guess you should say it was doing at least 15 miles an hour, maybe even twenty!. But what did the other driver have to say about it?"

"Well, it didn't actually have a driver."

"No driver? Great! A runaway vehicle, that’s even better. You should have no trouble at all with your claim. But how about the other vehicle, was it badly damaged? Was the driver Spanish? What did the owner say when he, or was it a she this time, arrived?"

"Darling, nobody did arrive. Nothing seemed to be wrong with it, so I just pushed the horrid thing out of the way and left it. Then I drove home."

"Oh dear, that doesn’t sound so good. You didn't get to exchange insurance information with the owner, but you managed to move it out of the way? What about witnesses, did you get any names and addresses?"

"Of course not dear, nobody wanted to know. The supermarket was closing, and I know the manager there doesn't speak English. Anyway, I don’t think it was damaged and they’ve got dozens more of them."

"Now just a minute, what sort of a car was it? How could you have possibly pushed it out of the way?"

"Well, actually it wasn't a car. It was one of those new shopping carts; the one's programmed to return to the store by themselves. Now don't look like that ... it really wasn't my fault. After I'd unloaded it and closed the boot of the car, I pushed the button on its coin panel, took out my money, and then sent the stupid thing back up that long slope towards the shop entrance."

"So, what went wrong?"

"It was the first time I'd tried one of those things and I wasn't sure if it was safe. So I followed it back up to the entrance to see if it was."

"Fine, good thinking … and was it safe?"

"It did seem to be, but the button light on it was still flashing and it wasn't quite home into the last one that was there, so I pressed it again."

"I see, but that should only have repeated the command to return it."

"That's what I thought, but the light was still flashing."

"So what did you do? Go in the shop again and tell them?"

"No. I just left it, because I thought it was safe enough there, and I wanted to get home, to get dinner ready for you."

"Of course sweetheart, but what happened? How did you get the damage?"

"Well, I thought it was safe, but on my way back to the car it passed me ..! It was moving quite fast, back down the slope. I was lucky it didn't hit me too!"

"Sweetheart, I don't believe this form fits that kind of accident. Think about your no-claim bonus. You weren't even in the car when it happened. Your shopping cart ran away, and nobody else was involved at all? Did you explain all this to the garage?"

"Of course not dear, I didn't want to look stupid!"

"Okay darling, I get it. Now I understand what this is all about. In that case, just tell them to send me the bill and let's forget about this form and the insurance. It's all too complicated. Yes love, I know that's what you were hoping I'd say … and I know I'm wonderful... how about an early night?"

This unlikely tale begins in Tenerife; but later, the unwanted stuff, it's all about, gets switched to somewhere distant, presumably in micro-seconds; but normally, even non-stop, it takes me about five hours flying time by passenger jet.

Set in the near future, it's one (improbable) way to solve a worrying municipal problem, which must be getting worse daily now. The first part resulted from an idea donated to me by Harry Harrison, that celebrated SF author, on one of his visits to this island. Incidentally, I actually wrote the last part of this tall tale a couple of years before that, but I since realised that it adds on here perfectly.

BLACK HOLE

Chapter One: Cause ...

"Yes professor, we have to do something about the horrendous garbage problem we have in this island. I invited you here for this free vacation, for you and your wife, because I read something interesting about your work at the university in Vienna. I believe it might have an important application here in Tenerife."

Professor Alfred Schneider raised an eyebrow, and rubbed his nose.

"Really, Mr. President, that's hard to believe? What has my work, with the international problem of radio-active waste disposal, got to do with you, in this pleasant island?"

"We have a serious waste problem here too, but it is only ordinary household garbage and industrial waste … nothing dangerous, just the expanding quantity of it that's the problem; more and more every day."

"Can you not dispose of it in the normal way; using landfill and incineration methods?"

The president glowered, stood up from his desk, and banged a fist on the top of it, hard. Then he smiled and sat down again.

"Sorry about that, but I've been under a lot of pressure lately. We haven´t enough suitable space left for any more landfill sites, and we can´t burn it, because that would upset the tourists. Have you ever tried to set fire to a plastic bag? This is only a small island, but we have a large population, for our size, especially during the tourist season; and we're becoming overloaded with the rubbish it generates. It's a real problem and we need help! What can you do for us?"

The professor sighed, and shook his head.

"I´m afraid you have been incorrectly informed about my work; as with so many other people. To put it simply, it entailed digging a very deep hole, excavating a large chamber to one side of it, and then lowering my machine down, and along, into it. It had to be a very deep hole, much further down than ever attempted before; and the machine is large and heavy. It was a very difficult project to complete, especially with so many so-called environmentalists objecting to it. You must have read some of their wilder claims; for example, that I was creating a new volcano? Then there's another problem; the machine needs a great deal of power to operate it, probably more than you generate now, for half the island. The whole exercise is very expensive."

"But, surely all that is because you are dealing with large quantities of hazardous radio-active waste? We don´t have anything like that here, or that complicated. I just want our, day to day, refuse moved to somewhere else."

"Where for example?"

"I don´t care where, as long as it isn´t to anywhere here, on this island."

The professor considered what he'd heard, and became thoughtful. Extra funds were always welcome, and there was still that research he needed to carry out, sooner or later regarding the long term effects of his machine. He smiled and assumed a confidential manner.

"The problem is Mr. President, the continuous use of a smaller version of my machine might have unforeseen consequences, I could not guarantee where the output would emerge. In the case of radioactive waste, we drop it a long way down into the interior of the earth. My machine already installed down there, creates what I believe is something like a miniature black hole, a safe distance away from it. The hole absorbs the waste, the intense gravity field compresses it and, the resulting concentrated weight, causes it to plunge itself further down inside the earth, down past the magma boundary, and probably right down to the earth's radioactive core. That´s the natural place for it and it becomes absorbed there, doing no more harm. In the case of a smaller unit, like the one my team built for trial purposes, the pseudo black hole we produced was absolutely minute, but the gravity field it created did partly produce the effect we needed, and confirmed my predictions precisely; but we had no idea where the output emerged. It was only a small test, and we didn´t used it for long. Just the contents of one small village's waste pit, which vanished completely over the week it took to remove it. Wherever the output did emerge, might not be noticed for some time, if ever. Nobody, anywhere, has reported finding it yet. One of my bright young assistants, who looked into it, claimed it could even have emerged out in space somewhere."

The president leaned forward, and held out his government chequebook.

"Good! I would like to buy that first model from you. Name your price! How far down will we have to dig the hole for it, and how long will it take to set it all up? We have some very clever people in our university, over here, and I'm sure, that with your kind help, they can do anything to it, to make it more suitable for what we need."

The professor shrugged, but he rubbed his palms together, at the thought of staying for even longer in this attractive place; and he smiled approvingly, as they began to negotiate.

Chapter Two: ... and Effect

Rudi Bockheimer lived near a small town not far from Vienna, in Austria. He was a bright young teenager, very observant, and always keen on looking into anything unusual. He noticed the strange phenomenon, late one rainy afternoon in October. It was still quite light, but the shadows were beginning to get longer. He was gazing out of his bedroom window at the time, which overlooked an extensive field, owned by the local farmer, who had been digging it over that morning with his large and powerful tractor. Rudi had watched it towing a formidable mechanical contraption fitted with dozens of vertical blades, with a twist in each them. He watched, fascinated as the machine turned the ground over, neatly hiding all traces of the wheat straw stubble left there before, after harvest time.

Then he noticed something very unusual. Not more than about two dozen paces out from his garden wall, he could see a small dark round patch. It seemed to be resting on the freshly ploughed ground. It looked as if someone had cut out a circle from some shiny black cloth, stretched it over a hoop of some kind, and then placed it on the ground. It didn't follow the contours of the earth surrounding it, the newly ploughed ridges effect. It looked very flat and mysterious and definitely was not there when the farmer had finished his work around noon.

Rudi, full of curiosity as always, at his time of teenage life, went downstairs, put on his anorak, pulled its hood over his head and then strode out for a closer look. He got within a few feet of the small black circle, then blinked in surprise, and paused warily. Something about the appearance of the phenomenon made him cautious. Its surface was inky black, but also shiny, and its edges seemed to be oscillating slightly, as if they couldn't decide whether to merge in with the upper or the lower parts of the ploughed up ridges in the sticky fertile earth.

Rudi got the impression that he was looking at a very deep hole in the ground, a black hole filled with water, about half a metre in diameter. He bent down to study it. It was certainly very black. He picked up a small stone and dropped it into the centre of the circle. He was not at all surprised to see it vanish, but the shiny surface didn't show any ripples. He tried another one, somewhat larger. That disappeared too. Thoroughly intrigued he returned back home and grabbed a long stick from the garden shed, the kind used in his mother's flowerbeds to support various large bushes.

Returning to the mysterious circle he gingerly prodded at it with the stick, near one edge. It went in easily, for about half the length of the stick, then he felt it come up against some kind of obstacle; and it stopped. Terry pushed on it harder, but it wouldn't budge. He decided to pull it out again, but soon discovered that he couldn't move it. Feeling frustrated, but burning with curiosity, he let go of the stick to see what would happen to it next.

Nothing did happen at first, then it began to slowly slide down further into the hole. Rudi watched it in amazement, as it also began to move sideways. Then, when it was almost across to the other side, it disappeared completely. Rudi felt a sudden urge, to step over into the circle. The feeling grew stronger, and he became apprehensive and afraid. He started to step back, away from the circle or hole, or whatever it was, but he found he couldn't. Something was compelling him to move forwards. He fought against it as hard as he could, but his feet began to slide relentlessly closer towards the edge of the sinister black circle.

He wasn't aware of actually stepping forward, in fact he was trying to step back, but nothing happened. His legs would not move and, to his horror, his shoes seemed to be sliding forward, of their own accord, and taking him with them, leaving twin furrows in the earth behind him.

Very soon, they had dragged him to the edge of the hole and begun to move relentlessly over it. He began to panic as he watched his beloved trainers beginning to sink down, taking him with them. He screamed aloud, but there was nobody around to hear him. His parents had gone out for the evening, and the nearest neighbours' house was half a mile away, further up the hill. Bending down, he frantically untied the laces of his shoes and tried to struggle out of them. Then he lost his balance and, yelling wildly, he fell down and over the side of the hole. He clawed frantically at the soft ground, trying to get a grip, but he only managed to pull handfuls of sticky earth towards him and into the hole, where it slowly vanished into the blackness. He glanced back down, and saw that his shoes had disappeared, and only the tops of his socks were showing. Then something soft seemed to grip him firmly by the ankles.

He felt himself forced backwards, as his elbows reached the edge of the hole. Sobbing madly, he tried to stand up, pushing himself with his elbows. Then suddenly, as his knees were beginning to disappear, the force dragging him down stopped pulling. Panting with relief, Rudi tried to lift one leg up out of the hole. It began to move slowly at first and then faster, as his fear gave him added strength. He twisted his body around and managed to put his shoeless foot over the edge of the hole. Then he shifted his weight over it and steadily began to pull out the other leg.

Moments later, he was out of the hole and staring down at it, wide-eyed. Something was lifting up out of it. A dark brown disk emerged, which soon turned into a small container, almost the same diameter as the hole. Slowly it rose higher and higher and then, as daylight appeared underneath it, it began to move sideways, slowly across the hole. Rudi's curiosity overcame his fear and he staggered around to the other side of the object to get a better view of it. It looked like it was made of some kind of tough plastic material. There was some large writing on its other side and, to his astonishment, he recognised it as Spanish, having recently taken that language as an extra subject, for his studies at school.

"Disposición de la Basura Científica S.L."

Then he noticed some smaller print, on it lower down.

"La Laguna, Tenerife."

He watched in disbelief, as the canister, slowly upended itself and tipped out a large heap of, what appeared to be, dark brown dust. Then it moved steadily back across to the hole, went down into it again, and disappeared. A few moments later, the black circle shimmered, faded and then vanished.

Rudi walked all around and over where it had been, but no trace of it remained. He picked up the garden stick and raked around the nearest edge of the heap. He tried to pick up one lump of something that looked like a very tiny model of a motor car, but it was unbelievably heavy. He decided his mother would be angry anyway, if it made a hole in his pocket, so he left it where it was. Scraping around further, he soon located his trainers, and after dusting them off, with some difficulty, he put them back on and thankfully went back home. After a hot shower, he watched TV for a while then went to bed, well before his parents returned home, much later in the evening.

* * * * * *

Next morning was Saturday, and he overslept as usual; but became disturbed by a commotion coming from outside his bedroom window. He got out of bed, rubbed his eyes and looked out. His father was there, still in his dressing gown, arguing with the farmer, who was pointing angrily at several large heaps of dusty looking material, scattered around his field. There was a strong breeze blowing, but it was having no effect on the dust at all. Rudi gaped at the sight for a few moments then wisely decided to go back to bed, and say nothing.

Here's another tall tale about an unusual visitor to the island. This one meets up with a foreign resident, who has already been here for quite a long time.

HIDDEN RECALL

There it was again, the strange looking lizard, although it was clearly not a normal Tenerife species of lizard. It was too big for a start, with a shorter tail, and its shoulder area was a strange mix of colours. The elderly hiker leaned over to get a closer look at it. It was something like a normal Tenerife lizard, at first sight, but he could see that it was different in several other ways; the most obvious being that it was wearing a little jacket, with its sleeves coming down to its elbows, in a delicate shade of green, with tiny yellow polka dots. Its front legs had longer, flexible, fingers on the end of them too. Very unusual indeed, and because he always saw it close by the pond, near the walls of that new medical company building, he thought at first it might be some kind of experimental pet that had escaped.

It sat still for a while, apparently just watching to see what he would do next. Keeping very still too, the hiker stared back. Soon, for some unknown reason, he began to develop a headache. After a while, still watching him, the lizard slowly backed away into the water, apparently afraid of him; not that he would have done it any harm, he happened to like lizards, and frogs and most little animals, but not people very much.

Eventually it disappeared and, at the same time, the astonished observer realised that his headache had suddenly ceased; surely not a coincidence? He decided the creature must have been something to do with it, and probably was afraid of him.

He went back there the following day, and there it was again; this time partially submerged. When he began to move a little nearer, it moved back the same amount. When he stopped moving, it stopped also. Very unusual behaviour for a lizard he thought. Then suddenly, a little voice came into his head.

'We really must stop meeting like this.' It said, in English, but with a German sounding accent.

The hiker was amazed. The same ridiculous thought had occurred to him too, at the same moment it seemed. Aloud, he exclaimed, 'Why not, what's wrong with that then?'

The lizard folded its front legs, raised itself up, and clapped its little hands together. The tiny clicks they made were remarkably penetrating in the still morning air. The small voice in his head answered accusingly.

'I don't like being watched while I'm bathing.'

'But you're a lizard.' the hiker replied. 'An unusual one for sure, but surely lizards like to go in the water, all the time.'

'When did I say I was a lizard?' argued the voice. 'I'm not, not even an unusual one. I'm a Prrstfthth.'

'What on earth is a … that?' the hiker queried. Trying unsuccessfully to mimic what she, the strange creature was clearly feminine, had said.

'Never mind,' Came the abrupt reply, followed by a pause. 'I suppose, in your language, you'd call me a camp-follower; but that's not very flattering!'

He thought about that, and replied, 'So what kind of camp are you following?"

She waved a tiny hand at him, and the little voice came again in his head.

'Our advance occupying force, of course, I'm expecting it at any time. I wasn't really supposed to come here yet, not until after it's all over.'

'I don't believe it.' The hiker said, nonplussed. 'This conversation is getting ridiculous!'

'You sound just like your father. He used to say that to your mother.'

'How on earth can you know that?'

'I can read everything that's stored in your mind, even things you think you've forgotten.'

'That's fascinating!' He replied, but aware that it was worrying too. 'So how far back can you go?'

'All the way, back to your very first words, even earlier. All the sights and sounds, everything you ever heard or observed is still there in your head. Your brain cells have an enormous storage capacity, but you don't appear to have the ability to access all your memories.'

'Yes, I read that somewhere once,' he replied, 'and we lose our short term recollections too as we get older, but some of our early memories start coming back. I know mine do.'

'That's right, it's a balance, it's only your recall functions that are limited.'

He considered that for a moment, and exclaimed, 'How come your English is so good?'

'I've learnt it from you. The German you can speak is also transparent to me. I can even understand some of the French, and Spanish, languages you learned at school too, but only as far as you got.'

All this was amazing. He wondered, could she also recall all the science and technology he'd learnt later. The voice came again.

'Of course! But thanks to my own superior education I can see what you've missed. Quite a lot actually!'

That was when he began to be worried. This little creature was clever and could read every one of his thoughts; quite a weapon in the hands of any invader. He felt he ought to warn the authorities, but would they listen? He had good reasons not to want to contact them anyway.

'You can't do anything to stop us.' The creature insisted, confidently. 'We're born rulers and we're going to control this island. It's all planned, and in a few of your days you'll see what I mean.'

'Assuming I'm not dreaming all this.' he said, 'Where are you from?′

′I believe you would call it another dimension.' She replied. 'Our universe is the opposite of this one. Yours is expanding outwards in time, away from what you call the Big

Bang. Ours is on the way back to another one. It's all part of the balance of nature.'

'I see.' he said. 'So you people want to move over to our universe to escape from your Big Collision, before it's too late?'

'Correct.' She said. 'And there's nothing you can do about it. There are too many of us, almost a hundred already! Any time now, we'll be here in our millions.'

That really got him worried. Hundreds, the island could probably manage and perhaps even benefit from the knowledge they appeared to possess; but millions were something else, and what about after that? He decided to learn more about the remarkable thought reading ability she claimed to have.

'Tell me about my childhood,' he said, 'something good that I've forgotten.'

There was silence in his head for a few moments. Then the voice came again.

'You fell asleep once on a bed of air. It was floating on that large pond you call the sea. The gentle rocking sent you dreaming and you thought you were flying through the clouds. You were very happy and not afraid. Then you suddenly awoke to find yourself in your father's arms. He had saved you from floating away.'

'Yes, I remember now, he held me very tight, and he was crying.'

'He said how much he loved you and would never let you out of his sight again.'

'Thank you for that memory,' the elderly hiker said, brushing away a tear, 'I'd forgotten it. We were never so close again, and grew apart as we grew older. He didn't agree about many of the things I came to believe in.'

'Yes that's very clear to me, it was the main reason you left home. You went away to be ready to join the big war.'

'Yes, I knew it was coming.'

'You have some memories there later that are not available to your recall process. They are not so easy for even me to see.'

‘I thought you could read all my memories, even if I couldn’t.’

‘Not all of them at the same time’, she said. ``Memories are like an old book with some of its pages stuck together. I can only read the open pages quickly. But you are trying to stop me opening the others.’ Suddenly she shuddered and shook her head. Her big eyes opened wider.

‘I can see you doing awful things, to other humans. How could you do that?’ She seemed shocked.

‘It was my duty! Situations like that have to be controlled.’ He insisted and closed his eyes in an attempt to close his mind, against the buried memories that had suddenly returned. He felt an urge to plea for her understanding.

‘I had to do it; it’s what soldiers must do. Obey orders, I had no choice, can’t you understand that?’

When he opened his eyes again, the little creature had vanished, without a ripple, as if she had never been there.

Next day he was there again, earlier, really expecting nothing; but she was already waiting by the edge of the pond. Her little voice spoke again in his head.

‘I’m really sorry, I have to go soon.’ She said, ‘It’s all over. The occupation has been cancelled, we’re going to look for somewhere else.’

He was at a loss to know what to say, but she wanted to explain.

‘Last night my Commander came looking for me. I told him all I’d learnt from you. He called all the other Commanders and they had a big discussion. Some of them had already entered the minds of other humans, elsewhere on your island, without them being aware of it. There were many reports like mine. They finally decided this world is too dangerous to take over. There are too many of you, and so big and aggressive. We really only wanted a peaceful occupation.’

‘I’m very relieved to hear that.’ he said, but feeling uncertain about what she meant.

She clasped her little hands together, and regarded him intently.

'My Commander said I should thank you for warning us, even though you didn't realize it. I can tell you're sorry for what you did in that awful war. Now that you're much older, you realize those things you did were very wrong. That's why you tried to put them out of your mind. What you did to other humans, because you thought they were different. Like other of your people would surely try to do just as much to us. We are even more different, our races could never be at peace.'

She was right and he knew it. Memories and remorse flooded over him as they regarded each other in silence. Then as she slowly backed into the pool, waving gently to him, the surface around her began to glow and shimmer. Suddenly she was gone, and he was alone with all his recovered guilty memories.

How ironic, the still agile old hiker thought.

"What I did all those years ago may have saved this island, maybe even the planet. But from what eventual fate I'll never know and how could I tell anyone even if I knew? Who would believe me anyway, a doddery ninety years old, and a fugitive, still indicted war criminal?"

There's an exciting rumour going around that a full-scale F1 circuit is planned to be built in the island ... so, the following speculative tale could be prophetic ... or maybe not?

FORMULA 1 EXTRA

I accelerated down the straight and began to catch up with Enrico again. He must have seen a problem ahead, because he suddenly braked, or was it deliberate? I knew I'd have to jump early to avoid him, but I didn't make it high enough and the damaged stabilizer caused me to tip partly over. My left rear wheel hit his video camera mount. The aerial must have penetrated the tire, because when I hit the track again, almost level, the resulting flat skidded violently and spun me around. The last thing I remember was the ground appearing a few times where the sky was supposed to be, then nothing.

I woke up in hospital with time on my hands, one of them anyway. I'm filling it in by dictating my diary. The word processor program on my laptop accepts speech input. I only have to get my little nurse to switch it on for me, and hit the right keys to start the program. She just did that, so here goes ...

We had to attend this secret briefing at the end of last season. The Big Chief, who owns everything to do with it all, told us drivers that the public was getting bored with the old style Formula One races. Whoever made it to pole position always won, because the circuits everywhere were mostly too narrow and overtaking was always difficult. The essential single Pit Stops were now so well organized, nothing ever changed. The same few drivers nearly always made it to the podium. The races weren't excting any more. Television viewers were switching off in droves and race attendances were falling off. What really worried him was the fact that the advertising revenues were nose diving, and it wasn't only due to the bans on promoting cigarettes and alcohol. It was clear something new was needed.

"So, the next season will be different," the Big Chief announced. "For a start, we're going to have a new cars and a new name, I think it'll be Formula One Extra. All the constructors have already been issued with the updated car specifications, and have been working on them secretly."

That was certainly news to us, and we all started to ask questions, but he waved us to silence and continued.

" The basic specification for the new cars is no different from the present, but with one important exception."

Then, what he said next made us really sit up.

"We're adding an extra engine, a high performance gas turbine. There's only one supplier involved, so each car will effectively have the same installation. It'll be up to you drivers to develop the necessary skills to take advantage of it, and the first trials will be held in Tenerife, where they've just commissioned a brand new track. I want you all to have a month there to get used to things, before the first actual Grand Prix event."

He smiled, at the startled gasps that arose from some of his audience, then continued.

"Until now we've kept this revolutionary news away from all you drivers, because we know how much you are subjected to pressure from the media. We didn't want anything to leak out until we were ready. Now, you're all wondering what the extra engine is for? Well, it's to drive four vertical thrust jets, one on each corner of the car. This means that when you want to overtake, you hit the button and jump over the car in front. There's also an automatic rear thruster, linked to the forward speed of the car at the point of takeoff. This means that whatever the speed you've attained, when you apply jump thrust, it will be increased enough to enable a pass to be made safely. In effect, the traction you lose when your wheels leave the ground, will be replaced by a compensating horizontal jet thrust."

He paused and looked around the rows of drivers. Nobody said anything, but their imaginations were working overtime. He smiled again and continued.

"Jumping thrust uses water, and the car design doesn't leave room for a large extra tank, so you must use it sparingly. It's injected into the exhaust manifold pipe, directly behind the turbine. The water flashes into steam and gives the extra thrust needed for lift and overtaking speed. It also cools down the exhaust considerably, for the benefit of the car being overtaken!"

A babble of voices interrupted him. He again waved them to silence.

"Yes, of course we've thought a lot about safety precautions! Everything is interlocked and fail-safe. However, there are some important points to watch. We've had to tighten up the rules for disqualification. As the new season progresses we may have to modify them further. I'll read you the summary of how far we've got, because no doubt the trials will give us reasons to add a few more. You can each collect a copy of this detailed list at the end of the meeting.

1. No jumping if a circuit has any low bridges. Monaco is definitely out! For the rest, we're arranging for all those arches that advertise tires to be removed.

2. You can't steer the car while it's jumping. So overtaking is only possible on the straight.

3. Beware of bends and sharp corners! No jumping to try to take a short cut.

4. No jumping before, or after, taking the pit lane.

5. No jumping to avoid being overtaken. If two adjacent cars are seen to be in the air at the same time, the one behind will be disqualified!

6. No jumping if you suspect you have any damage to your stabilisers. They'll act like aircraft ailerons and you may flip over. Make a pit stop as soon as possible.

7. Finally, and this is an obvious one, no jumping at all when the safety car is out."

I stood up and queried if it was in order to jump over wreckage, without going around it. The Chief's reply was affirmative, if you'd hit it otherwise, but all the video recordings would be scrutinised very carefully.

A few days later, my team mate Enrico and I were back home being introduced to our new cars. Trying them out initially on the factory test circuit was fascinating. My first attempt at overtaking Enrico went smoothly. I sped up to him on the main straight, then punched the jump thrust button. The car heaved up into the air and zoomed over him, with plenty of room to spare. A glance in the mirror showed him safely behind me, so I punched the drop button. The wheels skidded a bit as they matched my forward speed again, but I was still in control and soon snaked on ahead. The automatic controls had worked beautifully and the car seemed to have no problems.

Then it was Enrico's turn. He jumped over me successfully. We soon felt ready to play leapfrog around the track, apart from the bends, and that's exactly what we did for the rest of that day.

The first experimental race, on the new test circuit in Tenerife a fortnight later, was reasonably successful. However, the warmup-lap was a weird sight. We watched a recording of it afterwards. Some cars performed the usual left and right swerving manoevres, to run in the tires and give them more grip. Others, including me and Enrico, hopped up and down trying out the vertical thrusters. These antics certainly added another dimension to F1 racing and would surely prove to be more interesting to the spectators.

We had the usual startup glitches with the regular engines. Two unfortunate cars were left behind on the grid, when the trial race started. The ones behind them managed to avoid any collisions, mostly by going around them in the normal way. One of the stalled cars however punched his jump button, allowing the last of the cars, directly behind him, to continue on below. Turbines are more reliable than regular engines.

On the tenth lap, a potential accident was averted when one car blew its main engine. Its resourceful driver hit the jump button and stayed up until all the following cars were safely by beneath him. Then as the next bend came up, he neatly drifted off the circuit and landed in a convenient grassy field. The driver was fine and, apart from its engine, the car was undamaged. If the same thing had happened in the old days, it would have resulted in a nasty pileup!

The rest of the trials were uneventful, just a few minor scrapes and scratches. Probably because they were only trials and not really competitive. Nobody broke any circuit records. One day though the weather became untypical for the Canary Islands, it was rather windy and wet. When we jumped, our cars drifted sideways. This was inconvenient to say the least. After three cars left the circuit altogether, so nobody tried overtaking any more that day.

The first serious event though was a sensation. Thanks to some hysterical advance publicity, the circuit in Germany was packed, and the media loved it. Here's an edited transcript of my comments during the race.

"That pit stop was a fiasco, eleven seconds when it's normally only seven. Now I've lost position. Enrico, and perhaps one other driver must have passed me now. Yes, I can see Miki ahead of me. That means I've dropped back to third position. The main straight is after the next corner.

Now I'm gaining on him. He's already started slowing down ready to take the next bend. I'm faster that he is, so I can afford to move over. I'll let him go into it first.

That's distance enough now, I'm accelerating up to jump speed. Almost there, and only half way along the main straight. I've plenty of speed to spare, so here goes. Easy up and over. Great! He's throttled back to give me more room. The next bend is coming up so down I go again.

Wow! That was some skid, but I made it okay. Around the bend now and accelerating again. No sign yet of Enrico, and only three more laps to go.

Yes, there he is. Right at the end of the next straight, just going into the bend. I'm flat out now. Thanks for the message Jurgen. Yes, I thought that last lap was a new record. This one could be even faster! Next bend okay, very smooth actually. I can see Enrico nearer now. I must try to take him on this next lap. If not it'll have to be the last. Pity the finish line is less than half way along it. I might need more time to reach jump speed.

Damn it, he knows I'm after him. He took a chance on that last bend. Look how he slid around it. Nicely controlled, I'll give him that, but he cost me a few vital micro-seconds. Now I have to go flat out. It's this last lap or nothing.

Now we're level around the last bend. It was so tight I really thought I'd touched him. Maybe I did, but I didn't feel any damage, or see any on him.

Last lap coming up! I'm positioned about right, just enough behind him, ready for a jump. Foot down hard now. Damn it, he's trying to match my speed. But his car is slower so here I go. Punch the thrust button then up and over. But I'm not riding level. One of my nearside nozzles must have been damaged on that last bend. I'm beginning to tip over. Enrico is accelerating beneath me. Why doesn't he slow down and let me through? Now I'm well over, any more and I'll start plunging down again out of control.

Enrico must have hit his thrust button. He's riding up beneath me. We've collided now, but he's still coming up. The impact is levelling me up again. The indicator says my water is gone, I have to cut the turbine. Now we're locked together and that was the finish line and the chequered flag!"

Yes, Enrico and I made history with that race, and neither of us was disqualified. We locked arms and steadied ourselves together on what became the joint winner's level of the podium. Two F1 drivers in first place for the first time ever. Miki was second and Joni was third. That was some race, and the public was ecstatic!

The sixth Grand Prix event after that was the one where it all happened. There had been a problem with the track in Austria, where it was scheduled; because the race couldn't be held there, the authorities decided to hold it in Tenerife, where we'd had the first trial race. The authorities there were delighted. I was leading in the championship points table, but not by enough. I was also getting worried about Enrico. There were rumours around that he was seeing Erica. I didn't want to believe it, but more than once I caught her looking at him. The smile on her face was more than friendly. His was too.

I'd only made number two on the starting grid, but Enrico had made pole position. We had a good start, but he managed to keep ahead. However, I managed to pass him on the fifth bend, cleanly up and over, which seemed to make him really mad. He tore after me and, more than once, came so close that I felt sure our cars would collide.

Lap after lap we chased around the circuit, leaving all the other cars well behind. Eventually we were both ordered in for the inevitable pit stop. Enrico went in first, but the water technician blew it and he lost vital seconds. When I came out of the pit lane on the next lap he was soon after me, and going faster. He soon raced up nearer to me and started to jump. But I was already accelerating as fast as I could, and the next bend was getting closer. He didn't make it and had to drop back down again. I didn't like the way he shook his fist.

I noticed that he'd drifted across the track during that aborted jump, but fortunately into the bend. The wind was getting up. Then I saw another car beginning to lift up ahead of me. It looked like Miki jumping to lap one of the stragglers. I saw the wind catch him and drift him well over to the side of the track. He was unlucky, the barrier was lower there, but as he slid right over, he caught both his nearside nozzles on the top of it. The thrust immediately all went to the off-side nozzles and he abruptly flipped over. As I flashed by, I saw him bounce over and over and land upside down on what I believe was a kiosk serving tapas. I heard later that he did survive the crash, with nothing broken.

An extract now from my voice recording taken during that fateful race.

"Enrico is taking more chances, he seems determined to jump over me. We both broke the record on that last lap. I'm having to really drive, into and around the bends, now to frustrate him and stay in front. Damn it, he did touch me that time. My rear stabiliser is damaged! Now I daren't jump when I need to lap anyone and he knows it. We're on the straight again and he's jumping to pass me. I can't do a thing to prevent him ... Aaaaagh ....!!"

Things got a bit vague after that. I seem to have no clear memory at all of what happened. I know I tried to catch up again and pass him, but all I can recall are those visions of the ground, where the sky was supposed to be; and I remember thinking how strange the volcano, Teide, looked ... pointing downwards! The doctors here are very good, but they won't let me see a video recording of the race yet; nevertheless Jurgen smuggled me in a copy of the car's audio tape, so I could write this diary. I've smashed up one arm and have a badly broken leg, so I suppose my racing days are over. They tell me Enrico went on to win the race, and eventually the championship. He's never been in to see me though, and nor has Erica, which is sad, but I'm happy to report that I've just been offered the job of Technical Manager of the Circuit here in Tenerife, with a very nice new villa thrown in, going by the brochure ... meanwhile, I'm recovering fast and getting on fine here now ... especially with my latest little nurse. She speaks quite good English too, with a lovely accent.

In this life, if you look around almost anywhere long enough, especially here in Tenerife, you may well see something that appears unusual ... and you never know what it really might be, unless you go out of your way to investigate it.

ANCHOR LIGHT

It was another warm, moonless night when Juanita Rodriguez saw the strange light again. The elderly lady lived in a retirement home, part way up a hill overlooking a broad barranca. She had a cosy apartment, the end one of five, on the far side of the building away from the side road; with a balcony having a panoramic view, stretching away for kilometres. In the far distance, to her left and high up on one of the hills, there was an old ruined castle. She always sat out late, after her favourite TV News programme had finished, to watch the magnificent view. It was always beautiful and often different, especially when it was raining, and the lights in the little villages twinkled even more merrily. The rain never bothered her, there was a broad parapet roof over the balcony, which shielded her completely. Even if the wind was blowing in her direction, there was always a corner where she was protected from the rain. Recently, on two consecutive evenings, she had seen the strange light. It seemed to appear suddenly, high up in the sky and hover over one of the turrets of the castle, before slowly disappearing down into it, or perhaps behind it.

The first time, she had noticed it, she later put it down to her imagination; a trick of the light maybe. A car´s headlights reflecting off a window somewhere by the castle; not that she could see any other buildings, near to it, when she spent some time looking around in the daytime. She thought about telling someone what she had seen, but decided against it. It was her secret, and she was enjoying it, life in the rest home otherwise was, uneventful and, often boring, but how could she find out what it was she had seen?

Her son and daughter came to visit her the following afternoon. The time passed pleasantly and, far too soon, it was time for them to leave. Then her son had a question.

"Mother, is there anything we could bring you? Is there something you would like?"

It was her big chance. She seized it, and replied brightly.

"Yes, there is something I'd like. Do you still have that old telescope, the one I bought for you when you were a teenager?"

"Why yes, I believe it is still in a cupboard somewhere. You're right mother, I haven't used it for ages and it would be very nice for you here. That view from your balcony is fantastic. You'll be able to see the whole town on the other side of the valley, and everything else each side too; especially that old castle up on the hill over there."

He pointed to it enthusiastically. "What a good idea, we'll bring it to you next time, probably in the middle of this week; one of us should be free."

Her son was as good as his word, and turned up with the old brass telescope, two days later. His mother was delighted with it; she decided it was even larger than she had remembered. After she had cleaned the lenses, each end, her son set it up. When she was sitting down on the comfortable chair on her balcony again, he carefully adjusted the instrument's tripod to match her height. When they were both satisfied, he gave her a farewell hug and a reassuring comment.

"You don't even have to bring it in overnight mother, or even in the winter. I found the waterproof cover that came with it, and it's still in good condition."

She thanked him warmly, as he prepared to leave in a hurry. She knew he was anxious to get back to work again, and the traffic was difficult at that time.

Juanita spent the next hour looking around and across the valley. She was impressed with the telescope's clarity and magnification properties. Before long, the old castle leapt into view, and she could even make out the remains of some broken glass on one of the turret windows. She could hardly wait till the evening came, and it was late and dark enough, to begin looking for what she had seen before.

Naturally, life being what it is, that night nothing happened at all but, still reluctant to abandon her quest, she eventually went much later to bed than was usual for her. Same thing on the next three nights; however on the fourth night she was successful. The hovering light at last suddenly reappeared. Full of excitement she focussed the telescope on to it, as it descended over the castle turret again. This time she could make out the source of it more clearly.

It was shaped something like a large bottle, but on its side, with the glowing light coming from near its larger end. Then as she watched it, the strange object slowly turned over, until its narrow end was at the top. It paused for a moment, and then began to descend slowly. As it reached the top of the turret, and kept moving lower, the light from it became fainter. Juanita decided its glow was being blacked out by the turret, as the object descended further and soon vanished from sight. She thought perhaps it was some kind of helicopter, even though it was a funny shape? She was too far away to hear anything, and fast spinning rotor blades wouldn´t necessarily show up, even though it was a good telescope, she was using.

She went back into her apartment and sat down to think about what she had seen. The choice before her now was either to leave things as they were, or somehow try to visit the place. She was fairly active for her age, and could still get around; but there was no way she would be able to visit the place alone. She realised that someone would have to be let into her secret. She considered the idea for some time, then she remembered the young taxi driver, Rolando, who had brought her to the rest home in the first place. He would be the ideal person, and checking in her address book she found she still had his business card tucked into its plastic cover.

She checked her latest bank statement and decided she had more than enough money available, to cover the hire of a taxi for a couple of half days. With her mind made up, she finally went to bed and tried to get to sleep. It wasn't easy, her imagination was working hard; and when she did finally fall asleep, it was to experience strange dreams involving all kinds of weird flying objects and unusual occupants.

After breakfast, the next morning, and deciding to waste not a moment more, she put on her coat and hat and took the lift down to the ground floor. There was a telephone by the doorman's desk, at the end of the corridor, and she was soon asking the driver to call for her right away.

Fifteen minutes later Rolando drove up to the entrance of the retirement home. He helped her into his taxi, and after listening with interest to her story, was soon on the way to the old castle, where he parked the car, at the top of its driveway. The place looked abandoned and appeared to be deserted; its main gates were padlocked securely from the outside. Eager however, to discover what it was that the old lady had seen, Rolando suggested he should look around while she waited, in the taxi, for him to return. She agreed, reluctantly, so he got out and began walking around one side of the castle. Finding nothing of interest, until he arrived at a deep drop down to the dried up moat, and could go no further, he returned to the taxi. He gave the old lady a shake of his head, followed by a reassuring nod; then he proceeded to look around the other side. He had not gone far when, almost hidden behind some large bushes, he found a small gate in the wall, and it was partly open. He peered inside and, seeing nobody about, he ventured in through it.

There before him was revealed an extensive courtyard. It had a large lawn in the centre of it, which he was surprised to see was well kept, and there was a large lumpy looking object in the middle of it. He walked cautiously nearer, for a closer look, but suddenly became aware of his exposed position, so far out in the open. He became uneasy; as he realised that anyone, high up in the castle, could easily see him. He turned, went back through the gate, and hurried back to his taxi, to let the old lady know what he´d seen.

She could tell by the way he hurried towards her that he´d found something. She could hardly wait to hear what it was that he´d discovered.

¨What is it? What have you found?¨

"I found another entrance, and it´s been in use lately. I had a quick look inside, and there was a large object on the grass in the centre of the courtyard, but it was covered completely with some kind of silvery cloth and I couldn't see what it was. Yes, and there were some large dents in the ground around it. "

"I want to see it for myself,¨ Juanita exclaimed, clapping her hands together. "I saw it land there, like I told you, on several evenings. ¨

Rolando became thoughtful.

¨What I saw looked like some kind of machine to me, all covered up. I don´t think it was the same thing you said you saw. What surprises me, now I come to think about it, is that if something that big landed there more than once, it should have made a lot more dents in the ground than I saw there.¨

The old lady nodded in agreement, then she had a thought.

¨How many marks did you see there?¨

¨Just two, on the side nearest to me; but there could have been more, on the other side of the thing hidden from me." Then he joked. "How about if something with just one leg keeps landing there?¨

She took him seriously, and replied.

¨Maybe the thing you saw is something to keep it from falling over?"

Rolando gave her a funny look, and decided to change the subject.

¨Can you remember on what days you saw it?¨

"No, I'm afraid not. I didn't keep a record, but I wish I had done. I first saw it some time ago, then only on three occasions since then, and I've been watching every night for ages. It did look strange. The last time, through my telescope, I could see it was shaped like a large bottle, with lights all along it."

Rolando gave her a friendly shrug and grinned.

Ï wonder what it was you saw?"

"Perhaps it was some kind of UFO." The old lady exclaimed, sounding serious. "I've been reading a lot about them lately, it seems there are such things."

Rolando gave her a sideways look of disdain.

"I doubt it, and even if they do exist, why would one of them want to come here?"

"You never know, perhaps the creatures inside it want to set up a base here. Somewhere quiet where they wouldn't be noticed."

"But you noticed them, or whatever it was you saw!"

"That was just by chance, my balcony over looks the old castle; only four more of our apartments do that, and I know that their occupants all go to bed early and would never have seen anything that late."

"So what do you want to do next? I don't like the idea of you going in there. I had the feeling someone might be watching me, when I was nosing around just then."

"I want to come back here after it's dark, tonight, and go through that gate, like you did. Will you come with me?"

"Now look, you are not as young as you used to be, and it might be dangerous. Anyway, how do we know we'll see anything. You didn't see it every night did you?"

"No I didn't, but I've worked it out now. It happened three nights in a row, before, and tonight is the second night, so we should be able to see it."

He could see that her mind was made up, so he shrugged and agreed to pick her up again at around 11 p.m. Then he thought of a problem.

¨How will you get out of the retirement home that late? Don´t they close the doors when it gets dark?¨

¨Yes, of course. But I have a key to one of the side doors. I took the spare one they always left hanging up beside it. ¨

The driver accepted the inevitable and they drove back to the rest home, where he dropped her off promising faithfully to return later, as agreed. Much later, when they were back on the way to the castle, he expressed his apprehension again.

"It´s a very dark night, and the ground inside the castle is very rough. It will be hard on your feet, do you still want to go through with this?"

She was adamant, and gave him a determined nod.

"Of course I do, it´s exciting, and I have to know what´s going on up there. Don´t worry, I promise I´ll pay you extra for your time tonight.¨

He fell silent, the old lady was generous, and he needed the money, Christmas was coming, and his son wanted a new bicycle.

They arrived at the side of the castle, and parked the taxi. The driver had a powerful flashlight with him, and used it to show the old lady, the state of the ground she was walking over. She stumbled a few times, but he always grabbed her arm, and prevented her from falling, More than once she gave him a grateful smile, but it was too dark for him to see it. They reached the gate, the driver had found before. He halted and switched off his flashlight.

¨We had better go inside, without the light,¨he whispered, ¨We don´t want to be seen, if there is anyone about yet.¨

They proceeded through the side gate and, almost immediately, noticed a light on the far side of the open area. The driver whispered again.

"I think we should stay here. How are your feet?¨

"No problem," She assured him, "I have my stick, so I can stand up for quite a while if I must. Just a minute, I can hear something."

The sound was coming from overhead, a soft rushing noise, at first. They looked up, as it increased in intensity; until suddenly, a bright light flashed on and flooded the whole area. It dazzled them so much they had to close their eyes, and look away for a while.

The light became reduced, and they were able to to see a large mobile winch, with its support pads extended, in the middle of the lawn. The cable rising up from it was secured to a gigantic, transparent and flood-lit, object that was slowly settling down in the middle of the open area. Then a loud amplified voice suddenly thundered,

"What are you people doing here? You are tresspassing on a private testing ground for our new late night advertising campaign. Please leave immediately."

They gazed up at the object, open-mouthed as they both realised what it represented, from its familiar shape and the part of the lettering, illuminated from the inside, nearest to them.

It read ...

.... CA COLA
... ight is best!

With a couple of these tourist attractions already doing well in the island, why not room for another one, maybe up in the North East area?

MANSLAUGHTER?

Ellie Rogers was busy rinsing out the fish bucket by the side of the pool, when the pest appeared. She had just finished feeding her five dolphins and was looking forward to a quiet afternoon. The small dolphinarium was always closed to the public on Mondays, so that the essential weekly maintenance work could be carried out, without interruption. Pedro the slim, sleek and oily, part time pool attendant approached her wearing his usual slimy grin. He grabbed her by a sleeve and put an arm around her. She tried to push him away but he pulled her closer and leered expectantly.

"When are you going to be nice to me then?"

This time it was too much, Ellie became livid. She'd had more than enough of Pedro's daily advances, it was clear he believed he was irresistible, but Ellie couldn't stand him. She turned her head away from him and dropped the bucket, deliberately. It just missed his bare toes.

"Get lost you creep. How many times do I have to tell you? Leave me alone."

He ignored her protestations and tried again to put an arm around her.

"OK baby, how about a little kiss?"

That did it. She slapped his face away, with the back of her hand. The large green stone on her ring scratched him and it must have hurt. He cursed and slapped her back, hard ... twice! She cried out aloud in pain, and staggered sideways away from him. She made a grab for her expensive tinted spectacles, as they fell down and under her feet.

There came a sudden swirl of water in the pool as one of the dolphins abruptly turned and began to swim towards the feeding point. It rapidly gathered speed and, when almost at the edge of the pool, it leapt up out of the water and slammed its beak hard into Pedro's back. With a gasp he thudded forward into the wall and became impaled on the hook that was fixed there to hold the empty fish bucket. He struggled for just a few moments until his head slowly sagged down, and stayed there. After a few agonised twitches, his body became still.

Meanwhile, the heavy dolphin had flipped itself around and flopped back into the pool. Turning swiftly, with rapid flicks of its tail, it paddled itself higher, until it was halfway up out of the water; regarding Ellie who was crouching down and groping around to find her spectacles. Meanwhile, apparently satisfied that she was not any more in danger, the dolphin had dropped back under the water and was rushing back across the pool to rejoin the others.

After a few frantic moments, Ellie located and replaced her spectacles. She turned and recoiled in horror, when she saw what had happened to Pedro. There was no doubt he would never bother her again. Distraught and shocked, she ran along the side of the pool and into the manager's office. She picked up his telephone and called the emergency number for an ambulance. Once assured it was on its way, she called her chief at his home and blurted out the lurid details of what had happened. He was incredulous.

"What? You think Pedro's dead, and one of the dolphins killed him? Ellie, try and stay calm. I'll be there in half an hour, but I'll have to call the police first though. Don't touch him and stay in the office until I get there, and don't let the ambulance men take him away, if he is dead."

Twenty minutes later he arrived and dashed into the office. The ambulance had already arrived and the two amazed paramedics were still standing around examining Pedro, without moving him. Ellie was still in shock and hunched in the office armchair, with the telephone still clenched in her hand. The manager gently took it from her and replaced it on its console.

"It's me Ellie, you mustn't fret. It wasn't your fault. Stay here until the police arrive, they'll want to talk to you. I'm going to have a look at Pedro and hear what the medics have to say. By the way, which dolphin was it that attacked him?"

Ellie gazed up at him and shook her head.

"I .. I don't know. I'm not sure ... I lost my spectacles when Pedro hit me. Maybe it was Jay, or perhaps Louie. It was only trying to help me. It all happened so quickly."

A police car arrived and its two occupants marched into the office then out and over to the crime scene, Ellie had recovered enough to be able to follow them, assisted by the manager, when the detective in charge, insisted.

The patrol officer took out his recorder and activated it, as the detective began to question Ellie, already identified as the sole witness to the crime. After the second routine question, the detective's jaw dropped in surprise.

“What? Are you saying a fish came to the rescue, when the deceased attacked you?" He scoffed, regarding Ellie with a look of suspicion.

The manager butted in. "Dolphins are not fish; they're air breathing mammals, like us."

"Is that so, and she's saying the victim was deliberately killed by an animal?"

Ellie protested, still tearful. "I don't think it meant to kill Pedro, it only meant to just push him away from me."

The detective gave her a look of disbelief. "I've heard of a dog savaging someone who was attacking its owner, but never a dolphin." He turned and regarded the five playful creatures, busy chasing each other around the pool. "So, which one of them did it?"

"There's no way we can be sure." replied the manager, with a shrug. "But I suspect it was one of the three males."

The detective regarded the dolphins again and turned to the manager.

"The law here states, that if a dangerous animal fatally attacks a human being it must be put down, immediately." He drew his gun, and checked it carefully. "So I have to know which one it was, they all look alike to me. If neither of you know, then we'll have to examine each of them for any evidence. In this case perhaps, for any blood, skin or material fibres on one of them."

The manager snorted. "Apart from the problem of getting them to hold still long enough, those dolphins have been swimming around now for over an hour, since it happened. Anything incriminating would have washed off by now."

The detective sighed; he was beginning to sense that this was not going to be a routine investigation. "We'll have to try anyhow. The forensic team will be here any minute."

Another police car drew up and a couple of white coated technicians got out and were met by the detective. Together they went around the pool to inspect the body, listening in disbelief to the account of what Ellie had described. Once satisfied that Pedro was beyond help, the forensic technicians wandered around the pool to get a closer look at the dolphins. Eventually they returned to the detective and the older one shook his head. "Forget it! Any evidence on one of them would certainly be washed away by now, their beaks are glassy smooth and shiny. They're not called bottle-nosed dolphins for nothing."

The detective's face expressed his frustration, he pointed towards Pedro's body.

"What about the victim, surely there's the possibility of something incriminating left on him."

The senior technician shook his head.

"Not really, there's just a big bruise between his shoulders. The fabric of his shirt isn't damaged at all. It was the hook penetrating the front of his chest that killed him."

The detective scratched his head, and turned to the manager.

"It doesn't look like an accident to me. The question is, did the dolphin know what would happen. Did it know the hook was there and the victim was in just the right place for a shove to get him on to it?"

The manager gave him a derisive laugh, and scoffed.

"That's a crazy idea, you can't believe it. I guess the dolphin was trying to protect her, but where the victim ended up was an accident."

The detective turned and regarded Ellie.

"Are you sure you don't know which one it was that did it? Were you particularly friendly with one of them?"

Ellie shook her head.

"Not really, I think I love them all."

The detective had a sudden idea.

"Let's try an experiment. You call them over and see which one comes first."

Ellie went to the edge of the pool and made a whistling sound. As one, the five creatures stopped chasing around the pool, and each other, and headed towards her, in line. When they arrived, it was a dead heat.

The manager was surprised.

"What about that? I've never seen them do that before. Usually one or perhaps two of them get to her first, depending on how far away they are when she calls them."

The detective was suspicious.

"Is that so? Perhaps they're all in it together. Let's try it again from the other side of the pool, this time."

He led Ellie around to the other side, and was surprised, and annoyed, to see all the dolphins were following her, keeping close together. After an hour of this, backwards and forwards around the pool, and feeling even more frustrated, he gave orders for the premises to be closed until further notice. Satisfied that nothing more could be done for the moment, he watched the paramedics remove the body and load it into their ambulance. Then, with the patrolman in tow, he departed in disgust back to his headquarters, to report.

Later that night, Ellie was sitting by the pool, having given her charges their regular evening ration of fish. After looking around, to make sure nobody else was about, she clasped her hands together and gave out a small experimental scream. Immediately one of the dolphins broke away from the others and raced towards her. She could tell, right away it was Louie. He rose up out of the water and began to nuzzle her gently. She whispered to the large handsome animal, in a low soft voice. "Thank you Louie dear, for what you did to protect me."

She was unaware that the patrol officer, who had earlier managed to plant a bug on her jacket, was parked in his car outside the Dolphinarium. He was wearing headphones and his sensitive recorder had been switched on for some time. Satisfied, with what he had overheard, he started up the car and drove back to his headquarters.

Early the next morning the detective returned, and with him this time was another, grim faced, officer with a heavy rifle. The detective waved a paper at the dismayed manager.

"This is a court order, authorising us to destroy the dangerous animal known as Louie, for the crime of viciously attacking and causing the death of one Pedro Sanchez. We have it on record that Miss Ellie Burton has positively identified the guilty creature."

Despite the manager's protests, they left the office and went over and around the pool. Ellie was busy giving the dolphins their morning feed. The detective smiled at her and exclaimed triumphantly. "Right Miss Ellie, now tell me which is the one called Louie?"

She gulped in alarm. "Why him?"

"We know it's the one who killed Pedro Sanchez. We have a recording of you saying so, last evening. Call the guilty creature over, so that we can deal with it and close this case."

Ellie shook her head. "It won't work. He knows you're after him. He won't come. I'll prove it to you."

She went to the edge of the pool and called out the dolphin's name, twice. Nothing happened.

The detective became impatient. "Try it again, and give it your special whistle too."

Ellie did ... several times, but nothing happened.

The detective was close to losing his temper. He called the manager over, and demanded. "Which one of those five dolphins is called Louie?"

The manager shrugged. "I've no idea, I guess that's Ellie's pet name for one of them. Pedro might have known, but he can´t help you now."

The detective was furious. "We should drain the pool and shoot the lot of them. You'll be hearing more about this."

Frustrated and angry, he stalked off back to the car, followed by the marksman with the rifle.

The next day, after a short discussion with the company attorney, the manager decided to open the premises to the public again. Business soon became very brisk. The news had already got around, that one of the dolphins was a murderer, and the media loved it.

Later that week the detective appeared in the Dolphinarium office again, and asked to speak to Ellie and the manager together. This time he looked more cheerful, smiling broadly, as he explained. "You´ll be glad to know we've decided to drop things here. The forensic boys have reported back on Pedro's clothing and his DNA samples. They´ve found significant evidence to connect him with several unsolved crimes, including the death of that young girl in Santa Cruz last month. I guess we have to be grateful to your dolphin, whichever one it was."

Ellie laughed and spoke out loud.

"Did you hear that Louie ... you've been let off the hook." And she couldn´t resist adding, silently. "Like Pedro, when they took him away!"

There was a sudden loud splash from the far side of the pool as one of the dolphins leapt high up out of the water in obvious delight. The detective was astounded.

"Which one was that? Was it a coincidence, or can they understand English? But it was under the water; are they that clever? How could it hear what we said, under the water?"

The manager grinned.

"Some scientists think they can."

Ellie was in no doubt.

"I know for sure that some of them can even understand what we´re thinking, wherever we are at the time. I'm certain that really was Louie, he´s very good at it. Watch, I'll show you."

She called out, across the pool,

"Hi Louie, please show yourself, I want to ask you something."

One of the dolphins rose up out of the water, on its tail, and regarded her. Ellie gazed at it intently, for a few moments, then turned to the others again.

"I sent him a thought, asking him if when he came to my rescue, he already knew about Pedro and what he had done, and really meant to kill him. Oh dear … look at him now!"

They all gazed over at the pool. The dolphin was nodding its head, slowly, several times; then it dropped back into the water and began swimming around, energetically, with all the others again. However, at that distance none of the onlookers, not even Ellie, could tell which of the five intelligent creatures it had been, that had identified itself as Louie.

Afterthought ... how did I ever miss getting the detective to shout "Come on out Louie, we know you're in there" ...?

Items you pick up on the cheap might not always save you time and money. You never know where they've been!

DO IT YOURSELF

"Before you start painting that cupboard tomorrow Juan, I'm going to give you another pair of jeans. Those you've been wearing, for months now, are a disgrace. Look at them, all covered in paint, which won't wash out, and look at these holes in the knees. Your skin must show right through them now."

Juan's wife was doing the talking, so he accepted the inevitable.

"Well, if you insist, but I'll need them today. I've got permission to leave work early this afternoon; I can get a couple of hours painting in before tomorrow."

Juan arrived home early as promised. After a quick snack, he was ready to change into his new jeans. His wife handed them to him.

"What on earth are these? What a funny black material."

His wife replied proudly.

I bought them second hand, in the Playa San Juan flea-market, last Sunday. They were a quarter the price of a new pair, and look how clean and unused they look."

Juan held them up against himself.

"Whoever wore these before, must have been wearing stilts." He remarked scornfully. "You'll have to shorten them for me."

"Well love, I already tried but, there does seem to be a problem. My scissors won't cut the material."

Juan found that hard to believe.

"You're joking, I sharpened them only last week; what have you been cutting with them then, shoe leather?"

"No, nothing like that, my love. You try for yourself."

Juan took the scissors and studied them closely. He could see nothing wrong with them at all. He picked up one long leg and tried to cut the end of it. Nothing happened. He pressed harder until the scissors slipped sideways, and closed with the fabric squeezed between the two bent out blades.

Juan was astonished. He pulled the scissors out, with some difficulty, and examined them and the material closely.

"Weird that. Not even a mark on the material, and I'll swear the scissors are perfect. Now what am I going to wear? I suppose you've already thrown away my old ones."

His wife nodded glumly, but then she gave him a smile.

"You'll just have to roll the trousers legs up."

"Just like most of the kids around here do nowadays eh? I suppose you can always sew them up into position, if the material starts to unroll."

Juan began to put on the jeans. They were a bit loose, even though he was a big broad fellow. His wife bent down and began to roll up the trouser legs. Juan peered down at his shoes.

"Whoever wore these jeans must have been some size, at least two metres tall; and look at this heavy belt it's got with it."

He paused and gave her a puzzled frown.

"Hey, I can't see how to do up this funny buckle."

Finally though, he managed it. There was a sudden click and Juan vanished. His wife looked up in alarm and let out a shrill scream.

"Juan, Juan, where are you? Don't frighten me like this."

But there was no reply.

She gazed around the room in alarm; until suddenly Juan reappeared, with his belt hanging open. He looked bewildered, as the jeans began to sag slowly down to his knees.

"What happened, where was I?"

"Juan, you disappeared. One second you were there, the next you weren't. Then you reappeared, but not in the same place. How could that possibly happen?"

Juan was unable to shed any light on what had happened. He pulled up the jeans again and the zip higher.

"It must be something to do with this belt. The minute I undid it, I was back here again. It's certainly not like any normal belt; it seems to have a very strong magnet in it. Watch this!"

He brought the two similar looking ends together and immediately vanished … again. Then, just as his wife began a horrified scream, he suddenly reappeared.

"There you are, it happened; just like I said. There must be some kind of switch inside one of the ends."

"Oh Juan, you did scare me, but what was it like where you went?"

"I didn't have much time to look. I was too concerned with getting back. Come to think of it though, it looked about the same as here, but you weren't there. I looked all around but you'd gone, completely. That was why I returned in a different part of the kitchen. Something else I did notice. You know that big vase you knocked over, last week? Guess what! It was still there on the shelf!"

Juan had read a few science fiction tales and had often watched them on TV. He had an idea.

"This belt is something special. It must be very valuable to somebody. Perhaps its owner lost it, and someone else found it, and handed it in to the market, where you bought it? It works like magic. It either switched me into the past, or maybe into what's called another dimension, a parallel universe perhaps. I think I ought to try a few experiments with it."

His wife was aghast at the idea.

"Don't you dare try anything silly, Juan. I didn't like you disappearing like that. I don't think you should try it again. We should just get rid of it … hand it into the police, that might be best."

"I must try it again, and look around more. You come with me."

She was horrified at his suggestion.

"Never, but anyway that's silly. The belt isn't long enough; it only just goes around you."

Juan grinned. He pulled the belt right away from the jeans, and examined it carefully.

"You haven't looked at it very closely have you dear? Look, it can extend itself."

He grasped each end of the belt and pulled. It extended itself easily, but still seemed the same width.

"See! We can both get inside it now if we want. Come on, let's give it a try."

"No Juan! I'm scared; you never know what might happen. Suppose there's somebody there this time. If the belt belongs to them, they might want to keep it. Then how would we get back home?"

"Don't be such a baby! I won't let go of the ends, of this double buckle thing. If anything goes wrong, or gives us any kind of a problem, I'll undo the thing immediately; to bring us back here again, like I've already done twice now, with no problems. You really do worry too much. I think I know what I'm doing."

"Maybe you think you do Juan, but I don't."

They argued for about twenty minutes on and off, but Juan was determined.

"We could even bring back that vase you loved. The belt would easily fit around that too. Look how much you can extend it."

He pulled the ends even further apart. His wife had to admit she was impressed. She really did miss that vase. Her mother had given it to them, as a wedding present, and she was due to stay with them next month, for a long weekend.

She finally accepted the inevitable when Juan took her into his arms and proceeded to wrap the belt around them both. As he brought the ends together, it automatically reduced itself in length to fit perfectly around them. There was a sudden clicking sound.

"Juan, I think it worked. I can see the vase, but it seems to have changed colour. Anyway, let's get it quickly and get back home, please. I don't want to stay …"

She paused, as Juan interrupted her. "Surely it always was that light orange colour?"

"Never!" she exclaimed. “You know very well that it was more of a reddish brown."
"Like it is now." Juan grunted, looking amazed. “Look, it just changed colour. How did that happen and come to think of it, why do I feel heavier here, wherever here really is?"

They gazed around, and then looked up. Something else was definitely different. Apart from the vase perched proudly up on the shelf, the ceiling had vanished. All they could see now was blue sky.

Juan gulped, and his wife let out another shrill screech as two, unbelievably large and hairy, fingers came right down into the room and gently squeezed the pair of them even closer together. Juan tried to open the belt, but it was far too tight, and had already adjusted itself to the smaller circumference now required. Then, as they were being hauled up, and away, there came a deep rumbling noise, which they realized must be a loud voice from someone, or something … somewhere. There was no way they could know what it was saying, but translated for you, dear reader, it would be something like ...

“That holo-snare, on the end of the wormhole, has caught two of them this time. Our little son will be delighted. He was so unhappy when that other one escaped. But he really must learn that live pets are not just for the one day of his birthday.”

Finally, here's a much longer tale than usual, in three parts, and set far in the future. The first part concerns one well publicised way for a wealthy client to invest in an assured future ...providing it's not left too late. The second part is about a survivor of a worldwide epidemic, and the third part ties everything together ... right up to the end.

LONG TERM SURVIVAL
Part 1 – Frozen Asset

I don't remember my funeral but I recall thinking about it on waking up again this morning, or whenever it was. I could still feel the after-chill of the defrosting process that must have been successful, as far as I can tell at the moment. The necessary freezing technology wasn't considered very advanced at the time. I remember someone, with a very deep voice, saying that I had a good chance of survival. Because I was rather thin and bony, the freezing and eventual thawing processes would have a good chance of progressing successfully through me. Otherwise, any steep temperature gradients could be dangerous. The main problem would be in my bones. If the marrow inside them gets damaged, my auto-immune system could suffer and maybe even stop working completely. That could lead to all kinds of serious infection problems, assuming I eventually would be defrosted.

So I can only wait and see if everything does function properly. At least my brain functions do seem to be working reasonably well. I know my name. I'm Richard Alan Masters, aged 23 next birthday, and I can recall the start of the accident that led to all this. I was driving along the new motorway extension, about half way to Guia de Isoria, when my foot slipped off the brake for some reason and I can remember the strong smell of gasoline before the fire. They must have got me out just before the car exploded. I seem to remember a very bright flash of light and the heat.

I expect I did have a funeral, even if I wasn't actually there for it in person. I'm sure my friends and relatives would have been there. I wonder how many of them are still around now. I have a feeling I heard someone say it could be some time before they'd be able to revive me; possibly several years, fifty at least. I only have vague recollections of people talking, and doing things to me. The idea was to thaw me out when some future technology would be advanced enough to be able to put me right. So it must be that time now and hopefully I'm back to normal again! I wish this headache would go away. I must try opening my eyes next.

I panicked a bit at first because I didn't know then that it wasn't yet daylight. Then after a while I noticed it was getting less dark on one side of the room. I could see some faint light coming from a small window in the ceiling.

I've just discovered I'm able to move my left leg, which is very reassuring. Very soon I'll try the other one and then my arms. My head is much better now and I seem to be getting used to being alive again. I can see more now and I feel a lot warmer too.

At last I've managed to sit up. I seem to be wearing some kind of smooth body garment, but it's not light enough to see what colour it is or anything. If I can manage to get off this table, I wonder how long it'll take me to be able to walk properly again?

Well it wasn't easy, but not as difficult as I expected. I've walked up and down this room many times now and had a look at the other tables in here; five more of them altogether but they're all empty. There's a lot of funny looking machinery about. Lots of cables and switches and control panels.. There aren't any windows, except that one skylight in the ceiling, and I haven't found any lights or even switches anywhere yet. That seems strange really, but if there are any lights in here then perhaps they're switched on from somewhere else. There's a set of large doors, which might lead to some stairs, but I can't find a way to open them. They seem to be locked on the outside. There are also what look like the twin doors of an elevator, next to them, but when I pressed the buttons, on the wall between them, nothing happened. There's a small room at the far end of this one. It's some kind of office with a small table and a chair. There's a funny shaped telephone on the table, but it doesn't seem to work. I think I really must find a way out of here. I tried shouting for help, but nobody came. I don't understand why, but my voice doesn't seem to be very loud, even though I shouted as hard as I could.

If I take the chair and the table from the office, and pile them up under the skylight in the ceiling, I might just manage to climb up and get it undone.

I should be exhausted. The skylight was at the bottom of what seemed to be like a very long chimney. The bricks, it's made from, were rough enough on their surfaces for me to be able to climb up them. Using a foot each side, one after the other, it seemed to take ages for me to reach the top. I had to be very careful not to fall back down. I never did like heights. Now it's getting dark again and I can't see anything much. The chimney opens out on to what must be a flat roof. It probably won't be very comfortable, but I think I'll stay here until it gets light again.

Well, it's daylight again and I'm confused. That room I woke up in yesterday really must be some long way down underground. I do seem to be on some kind of flat area, but it's not a proper roof. I think I'm still underground. The only light seems to be coming from somewhere over to my left, but much higher up. At least I'm warm enough down here.

At the far end of the flat area, I found another room which seems to be some kind of store. There were lots of boxes of all kinds of things on some shelves. I couldn't find anything I could try to eat right away, but then I wouldn't say I feel hungry.

Next to the store room there's a metal ladder, leading up to from where the light seems to be coming. I went up it and found another flat level with a big window overlooking some spiral stairs leading even further upwards. The window isn't made from clear glass, so I couldn't see anything on the other side of it. There seems to be even more light coming from higher up, so I've decided to go on up as far as I can.

It's a long way up this spiral staircase. There are sets of doors on each level, which must be for an elevator, but I can't open them. That room I woke up in must be a really long way below ground. It's much warmer now and the light seems to be getting stronger too. It can't be much further up to the top.

I've just about got over the panic feeling again. At the top of the staircase I found where the light was coming from. I'm on what looks like a big open balcony overlooking an endless desert of orange coloured sand! There's only one floor above where I am, but with no windows. The light is coming from what looks like the sun, but it's a funny colour, a kind of dark yellow. Perhaps that's due to all the dust from the desert. It's even warmer up here, but not too uncomfortable. There's a big staircase going down from the balcony, leading out to the desert. The handrails go right down into the sand. Perhaps there's more of it now than there was when the building was constructed?

I was hoping to find some people about, but there's nobody and it's so quiet. I had a good look at myself just now. Not with a proper mirror, but a reflection in one of the big windows on this level. I seem to be slimmer than I remember I was before. This one-piece suit I have on seems to be all over me, gloves as well. It's very comfortable and my shoes seem to be part of it too. It all seems to be tightly fitted and made from a very strong material because I can't seem to lift up any parts of it. I've just realised that although I must have been alive again for nearly two days now, I don't really feel hungry or thirsty.

That's very strange, as well as this feeling that I'm a lot slimmer and taller than I was before.

I decided to go down the staircase to the outside. I spent some time in jogging around, but there's nothing much to see; just a lot of black sand, and lava stretching away everywhere as far as I can tell. On this side of the building anyway, right to the horizon. The building itself is very wide. It's joined to a high wall on both sides, stretching away as far as I can see.. I don't feel like exploring all the way along it so I think I'll go back inside the building again and see what else I can find.

I'm just about getting over a big panic attack. Going along the front of the building and back in again at what seems to be the main entrance, I came to this large room. There's what looks like a big main control panel, with a large screen up on the wall in front of me. It shows a map of the area and all kinds of information. The islands look a lot smaller than I remember, and there seems to be a lot of little ones. But down in the right hand corner it reads ... 07.08.2177 ...! That surely can't be right, but it's got me thinking about how high the seas were predicted to rise from the effects of global warming. At the top of the screen the words - ***Investigate Power Malfunction in Elevator 3.5*** - are flashing very slowly. The Spanish translation of them is displayed underneath too. I've no idea how to do that, but it certainly explains the problem I had, in getting out from that room where I originally woke up.

I've spent some time trying the buttons on the Control Panel. Just touching them makes things happen. One of them shows layout plans of the building on the screen. I soon found a plan of the room I woke up in originally. It shows all the tables I saw and they had names on them. Mine was marked 17 and flashing red, but all the others had a heavy black border. There seems to be a lot of other rooms with tables arranged in them too, but all with black borders around the ones that do have names on them.

I just found the plan of a smaller room with only two tables and both of them have names coloured in green!

It's taking a lot longer to find that room than I thought. All the doors open easily from the outside and I make sure they don't shut automatically, using a piece of metal pipe I found. I'm on the other side of the building now, but only down about four floors. There must be hundreds of rooms in this place, mostly empty, but the ones on this other side are different. Smaller for a start and with special windows, that appear to be looking out over the back of the building, even though they really must be underground. The view is very interesting and nothing like the volcanic desert on the other side. Palm trees, a lake, small fields with plants growing … it looks like paradise to me, having been brought up working hard all my life before, in a big polluted city. Way in the distance I can see what may be the sea, when the weather is very clear.

I'm overjoyed! I've at last found the room with the two tables and there are children on them, a boy and a girl. Both of them are tall, blonde and very beautiful. The girl looks about thirteen or fourteen years old, and the boy perhaps a little older. Each of them is resting on a padded table under a long clear plastic cover. Their faces are completely covered, by small masks. There are all kinds of other connections and cables and panels around them. The rest of the room is full of complicated looking equipment too, most of which seems to be working quietly. I'm not sure what I should do next. I just want to keep looking at the children. They are both so attractive and apparently alive and breathing regularly. But I'd better not interfere with anything.

Two more days have passed since I found the children. I've been exploring the Oasis, or whatever it is. It's a marvellous place, fertile and very large, although I haven't been to the end of it yet. I think the desert starts again further out, going by the way the sun looks darker in that direction, but right in the distance I can see what looks like the sea again. In the other direction, when the weather is really good, I can see what looks like a volcano. It must be Teide, but it doesn't seem as high up as I remember it.

There are all kinds of fruit growing on the trees and bushes, and several small machines on legs moving about. They must be doing the gardening, the place needs, and looking after everything. It's all very strange here, but somehow I'm not really interested in trying to interfere with anything. I get the feeling I'm waiting for something important to happen.

Something unusual has clearly happened to me since I was frozen. I keep going over these thoughts I have, they're like notes in a diary. I remember them all, every word, right back from when I first woke up. Clearly I'm different from how I used to be. This blue suit I'm wearing seems to be an integral part of me. I think it's made from a new kind of plastic, maybe it's even metallic, or a mixture of both. I don't get tired any more now, not like that first day, but when it's dark I seem to slow down after a while and stop thinking, which is the only way I can describe it. Then I wake up with a start just before it begins to get light again. I think it's about to happen to me again now ....

Now I have learned everything, and know what I've become. I was in some kind of shock at first, but since then I've got used to what I believe is going to be my future here. The children woke up this morning. They raised their arms and lit up the control panels over their heads, within a few moments of each other. Their masks lifted away, up with the connections and the clear covers, then they both sat up and yawned.

The girl looked at me first and stretched out her arms. She smiled warmly and then spoke to me in Spanish. That was a shock, I didn't know I ever knew the language, but I do recall how I always did plan to get down to it some day though.

"Dear Father, is it really you?" She said.

I was stunned, and could not answer. What did she mean? Then the boy got off his table and stood up.

"Of course it's not." He spoke scornfully.

"It's Joseph Seventeen, he was English. I was told he'd be here to look after us, he was the only one who survived. None of the other cyborgs were successful, they were mostly too old." Then he turned to me and ordered, "We'll soon be ready for lunch in the Garden, Joseph. You'll find our day clothes in that big cupboard, over there by the kitchen."

Part 2 - FUTURE PERFECT?

I arrived at this Paradise Island about a week ago. It's better than I expected. Every comfort and my own servant on hand, always ready and willing, to do everything I could possibly want. The dome provides a perfect climate and even extends out over part of the sea. I'm never keen on getting wet, but it's pleasant to paddle around when I'm in the mood. There's only the one beach though, because everywhere else the island has steep cliffs plunging down into the sea.

Food and drinks are provided automatically, either in the dining area or in the hut by the beach. There's a wide choice and everything is always fresh. Anything I leave, even on the ground, is promptly collected up and presumably recycled. There's never a sign of rubbish anywhere. The whole place is immaculate and impressive. The servant comes around regularly with a large trolley and clears up everything. After all I've been through, getting here, it's great to relax. The servant adopted me on sight, immediately wanting to know what it could do for me. I only had to mention that some food and drink would be good and there it was.

It's been a long time since I left the Institute in Villaflora. There was nobody about when I finally woke up back there. The temperature had gone up even higher and most of the supplies had gone. I suppose the others had finally left for somewhere safer. I remember how shocked they were to discover that the missing technicians had taken the helicopter, the two unkind ones. One of the others, Carlo who was always good to me, had left a note saying I should try to find the owner's island, where I'd be safe. He'd drawn a little map and left my name on the envelope in very big letters, I suppose so that I wouldn't miss it. They must have been in a horrible panic and decided not to take me with them, thinking I'd be too much of a burden in my condition.

I decided I should leave too, taking what little food was left, heading away from the sun. It soon proved to be a very difficult journey for me, once the shady trees gave way to mostly desert. The further I got the more bodies I saw. Occasionally by the roads and in the otherwise abandoned buildings. They looked like some kind of disease had hit them. The situation had me scared at first, but as the days passed I decided I must have become immune to it, whatever it was. It must have been that vaccine I agreed to let them try out on me. More than once I remember they said it was their last hope. So it must have worked, but perhaps they didn't have time enough time to manufacture more of it. I haven't seen any other survivors since I began my journey. The servant I found here doesn't count of course, it's certainly not human.

The journey really was difficult. I traveled mostly at night when it was cooler, and also in case I did meet up with anything or anyone dangerous. I think it took me about ten days to reach the coast. I knew the island must be somewhere to the East after that.

When I saw the remains of the helicopter up against a large rock on the beach, I knew I was going in the right direction. Those two bad laboratory technicians were in it, and very dead. It looked like the disease had got them before they could even reach the refuge island.

After two more days, I saw the little island at last, but how could I get out to it? I spent the rest of that day wandering up and down the beach and thinking about what to do next. Then, just before it got dark I found a half-sunken rowing boat, but with a large hole in it.

After a restless night, halfway up in the branches of a tree for safety, I'd worked out what to do. I collected as much wood and big leaves as I could find and stuffed them all in the bottom of the boat, under the seats, so that they wouldn't move. It took a long time, but finally the hole was sealed up. Enough of the water became displaced to allow the boat to start rocking gently. The wind was blowing on to the shore, so there was no danger of the boat drifting away. I used my cupped hands to tip out more of the water that was left.

I'd seen pictures of boats at the Institute and sometimes in films. I'd even seen people rowing them. I needed to make some oars, but all I could find was one long stick and a small flat piece of wood to fix to the end of it, using some old thin rope that was still attached to the boat. It was all I could manage that day. Worn out, I decided to stay the night in the boat and see what to do in the morning.

I awoke early and was horrified to find that the boat had floated away from the shore, with me in it. The wind direction had changed and I remembered the water level going up and down during the day. Not a lot but, because I had made the boat almost float when the sea was at its lowest level, in the night when the wind changed it was enough. Even with my extra weight.

I saw I was drifting towards the island, but would miss it if I didn't do something. I tried rowing with my oar, just resting it on the side of the boat, but it only kept slipping and making the boat spin around. In a panic I thought I'd have to try swimming for the first time ever, as much as I hated the idea. Then I thought about putting the oar into the small notch I noticed at the flat end of the boat before dipping the blade end into the water. I soon discovered that moving the long stick, from side to side, made the boat point different ways and sometimes in the way I wanted. But it didn't seem to be really moving in the direction I needed. Then I accidentally twisted the stick just as I was moving it sideways. I felt it grip the water and was sure the boat did move forwards. I realised that if I twisted it the other way when I moved it back, I should get another push forward. I felt very proud of my reasoning when it really worked.

Some time later, with the boat well under control, I came up against the wall coming out from the cliff on one side of the island. I managed to grab a rope that was hanging down from it, next to a ladder. Climbing up and very glad to be back on land again, I found I was on the edge of a flat open space with a big letter 'H' in the middle. There was a door in the cliff, which I ran towards, only to find it closed against me. Just like some of the secure doors back in the Institute, it had a panel with push buttons on it. Sixteen of them, marked from 'A' to 'P'. I tried pushing some of them but nothing happened.

I sat down to think and then remembered the note Carlo had left for me with my name on it in big letters. Carefully I spelled it out, pushing the right nine buttons, one letter after the other. It worked! The door swung open and I was soon inside a long tunnel, with sets of stairs going up and up. It quite a long way to climb for me, in my condition, but when I emerged into the open at the top, there before me was the servant, but nobody else anywhere at all.

So, it seems I could be the only survivor. The once proud human race may be gone; but I'm alive here in this very comfortable place, this millionaire's paradise. I've decided to spend the rest of my days here and enjoy every moment, with my twins when I have them. The servant will help me. I deserve a good life after all I've been through. That painful serum they injected into me back at the Institute, then all the different drugs and vaccinations. Before that, there was all that processing to make me more intelligent. A lot of good it did for them! But I must be grateful. It has certainly proved good for me, little Columbine; the world's first, and hopefully not the last now, genetically engineered and very pregnant, chimpanzee.

Part 3 - Epilogue

I've been awake here just over fourteen years now and I enjoy my new life very much. The children soon grew up, and their first child was born last year. A beautiful baby girl, they named Daniela, with black hair like her Alyssia her mother, and green eyes now like her father, Alexis.

Now Alyssia is pregnant again. They want a boy this time, naturally. They seem to be able to make sure they will, using some technology that's beyond my simple understanding. After all, I'm only a resuscitated cryogenically frozen accident victim from way back in the twenty-first century. I suppose I´m almost what used to be known as an android, from what Alexis told me; that's better than being called a cyborg.

'Joseph, you're more than half artificial.' He said to me once. 'But we love you anyway, the best part of you is still human.'

I occasionally look at myself in a mirror. My metallic blue one-piece suit is very elegant, and is still self-cleaning. I don't have any hair, unlike Alexis whose blonde locks reach down almost to his waist, but that's not important. I'm always clean-shaven though, wherever it would otherwise show, without having to do anything. My eyes are blue, just like newborn babies' always are. Funny thing though, I seem to remember that, before my accident, they were brown.

Our life here in the big garden section of the building is idyllic. I keep everything in order, with the help of the little gardening robots, while Allysia does her painting, and Alexis composes and plays his music. He's in his Mozart period now. He rearranges all the complex orchestrations, and plays them, on his synthesiser. Some of his more intricate arrangements are beyond me. I prefer lighter music, but then I remember back in the old days before my accident I was still keen on the music of a group called the Rolling Stones, or was it the Beatles? They were still popular back then, even though it was over sixty years since the last of the group passed away. There's a vast library here of all kinds of recordings. I often play some of them when I've enough spare time, usually that's at night.

Quite some time has passed since I recorded those last notes. There were complications with Alyssia's pregnancy. Tragically, she didn't survive the birth of her son. There was absolutely nothing I could do to save her. Poor Alexis was distraught. He played nothing for weeks, and just went for long walks over the sands around the top floor of the building. I often tried to console him.

The boy Angelo grew up fast and healthy, but lonely. He had nobody of his age to play with. I was a poor substitute, but better than nobody I suppose. Daniela looked after him too, and I guess the two of them soon became close, once Angelo became old enough. I helped bring their twins into the world. Two lovely girls though, named Jan and Meg. By then Alexis had grown quite old, but he still had his music.

I get on fine with the twins. They're very energetic and love to play games. I often join in, being still quite athletic. In fact I don't seem to age at all. My processing must have been perfect. I remember Alexis mentioning to me that I was the only cryogenically frozen patient to survive and complete the process. That thought continues to make me feel very special. I feel very grateful towards the doctors and technicians, long gone now though, who made my continued existence possible.

But back to the music situation; one morning I heard something familiar being played. I recognised that it was a Beatles song, called 'Yesterday'. The twins were playing it. They'd found the complete collected works of every group that ever recorded anything back in the 1960's. They often play them, because they know I enjoy them too. Alexis though, usually complains about the noise if his study door is open and he hears them.

Yesterday he came out to protest about the noise, but it wasn't from music. It was the chimpanzees again. They make a terrible racket when they come to see what we're doing. It's hard to understand what they're saying most of the time. They've apparently evolved a changed dialect over the years.

Alexis and I once took the helicopter flyer out for an exploratory trip, once I got it going, and discovered their home island. It was rather crowded with them, but they didn't object to our presence. They were even quite helpful. One of them showed us their library. In it we discovered a recording left by the mother of the very first babies born there. She had apparently found the island, and its robot servant, after escaping from the genetic research establishment where she had been imprisoned. Apparently her name was Columbine, and she was very clever and resourceful. We learned that she had lived for a long time after they were born. She couldn't have any more babies, but her twins could. Quite a colony of them built up over the years. Too large by the time we got there. It showed in the way they were always quarrelling and fighting with each other. Their robot servant was constantly separating them.

After we'd looked around enough, we just left them to it.

The following year Alexis died, peacefully. He was very old. I buried him in the garden, next to Alyssia.

After that sad event, nothing important happened, and time passed uneventfully again. Then a few years later, two different chimpanzees came to visit us. Their robot servant drove them here in a strange looking three- wheeled vehicle, which must have been amphibious to get to the coast from their island. We entertained them as best as we could. They certainly enjoyed the bananas growing on the trees in our garden. We let them take a whole bunch away with them.

There was no more contact for a while, until one day some more of them arrived to see us. This time it was a visit by seven of them, three males and four females. The robot servant was driving their vehicle again, and it was towing a small cart with the females in it. The cart looked like it had been made from an old boat they'd found somewhere. It didn't have any wheels at all, it just slid along on its keel. Clearly their strange, three wheeled, vehicle was powerful enough to tow it.

It took me some time to discover that they needed our help on their island. Most of the colony had died, apparently from some unusual illness. It might be something mutated from the remnants of the disease that, long ago, must have wiped out every other living creature in the world. That is with the exception of me and the original children, and that female chimpanzee who found the island refuge. I often wonder if anyone else is still alive elsewhere in the world.

We agreed to come and help them. The twins and I loaded up the flyer with medical supplies and we departed. We got to the island later that day, well before the returning chimps of course.

We landed on the dome with the big H sign still visible on it. Then we had a look around, only to find the place almost deserted. There was no sign of the older residents we'd seen the last time. Just a few very young ones, looking helpless and unhappy. Some of them were even crying.

We unloaded the supplies and soon set up a makeshift hospital in one of the rooms, under the main dome. Somehow, just as in previous but usually minor emergencies, I seemed to know instinctively what to do. My programming must have been very thorough. I picked up one of the very young ones and ran an analysis, with one of the instruments we'd brought, but had never needed before. Up on the screen came a result, indicating it was a mutated form of the original virus that had decimated the world. There was also fortunately a prompt option to see what to do about it, which I took. A new page soon appeared, the first of several with a lot of instructions. I suggested the twins turn in for the night, as it was getting late. They agreed.

I worked on during the night, having never needed any normal rest, since I awoke from my cryogenic sleep all those year ago.

Not long after daylight, the twins called me to say the chimps′ vehicle had arrived on the beach near to the island. It was about to drive into the sea and come out to the island. I went up to watch it.

Half way over, the boat with the females in it began to sink. The robot servant became very agitated. It clearly didn′t know what to do. I dashed over to our flyer and lifted it up and across to the stricken boat. I just made it in time as the sea came over the gunwhales and the female chimps tried frantically to climb out and hang on to the tow rope. I set the flyer to hover and lowered the cable from the winch. Three of the chimps grabbed it one after the other and climbed up into safety. Unfortunately one of them, the eldest, didn't make it. She and the boat vanished completely under the water, and the weight of it began to tip up the amphibious vehicle.

The robot servant became even more agitated. Clearly it had been programmed to avoid contact with water, especially sea water. I hadn't as far as I knew, so shouting to the robot servant to let go of the tow rope, I leapt out of the flyer, which had already compensated its height over the sea as each of the female chimps had grabbed and climbed up the cable. I soon found the half-drowned chimp and towed her under the hook at the end of the cable. It was just out of her reach, so I kicked my legs and rose up enough to grab it. Thankfully she gripped my feet, then crawled up to perch on to my shoulders as I climbed up and into the flyer again.

The robot servant brought the amphibious vehicle safely alongside the jetty at the base of the landing platform on the secondary dome. I had already landed by then. We met up with the others inside the main dome. I rejoined the twins and we carried on with the hospital work. A week later, all the illness symptoms had vanished. The chimps were very grateful and sadly waved us goodbye. All that is, with the exception of a baby female one, who had lost her parents. The twins brought her back with them, and called her Columbine, after that first distant relative. She soon learned to chat away intelligently, and grew up to be very clever.

Many more years have passed since that exciting episode, and we´ve all grown closer together. The robot servant can't actually talk, but we're able to communicate by tele-screen now. We get on well and, every now and again, we visit each other together with a few of our charges. It makes a nice break for us all, a change of scene, and the chimps love our bananas.

Even later now, there are almost equal numbers of chimpanzees and humans. Each couple only ever has two babies when their time comes. The chimps seem to have lost most of their hair, and the humans seem to have grown theirs more. Over the years, I've noticed how alike they've all become, especially the babies each new generation still manages to have. But perhaps it's just me, maybe my eyesight is not what it was? I must be very old by now, and I can't believe I'm going to last forever.

About the author.

Tony Thorne MBE is an Englishman, born and technically educated in London, England, but now living in Austria and, in the winters when he can, in the warmer Canary Island of Tenerife. He originally qualified as a chartered design engineer and subsequently created a well-known British company (now American owned) specialising in Applied Physics products.

For developments in the field of low temperature (cryo)surgery instruments, and very high temperature furnaces, for processing carbon fibre, among other things, the Queen awarded him an MBE. Later he emigrated to Switzerland where he created, and became CEO of, the European Division of an American Corporation specialising in medical laboratory, and computer-related, products. Much earlier in life he, also wrote science fiction and humorous stories, was an active SF Fan, and a spare time lecturer for the British Interplanetary Society. He has since written papers and articles for several technical publications, and has held patents, in such varied fields as nuclear protection clothing, very high temperature processing, and microbiological assay laboratory equipment.

After many subsequent business adventures, including the pioneering development of AI computer software for business applications, he is now an enthusiastic author of quirky speculative fiction, mostly tall Science Fiction and Macabre tales, with over 90 short stories on file.

His personal website is on … www.tonythorne.co.uk

Tony Thorne MBE's SF & Macabre, and other publications, so far, include-

TENERIFE – Tall Tales with a Twist (Whortleberry Press, USA), TALL TENERIFE TALES, MORE TALL TENERIFE TALES, FUTURE REASSURED, and FUTURE UNCERTAIN (Etcetera Press collections)

Satire - HOW TO BE A TOP EXECUTIVE, THE QUALITY OF LIFE, THE JUNIOR PHILOSOPHICAL SOCIETY (Etcetera Press)

Poetry - SECOND OPINION [The Poets Yearbook], SHOWCASE –The Guernsey Poets, (Editor & contributor), and the websites AUTHOR'S DEN, and SCIFINITY.

Plus Stories, Poems & Articles in various magazines and anthologies, including FICTION-ONLINE, PLANET, NEBULA SF, THE BRITISH SF MAGAZINE, CATS AROUND THE CHRISTMAS TREE, CREATURES OF GLASS & LIGHT (EuroCon2007 anthology), AXXON (Argentina), SPICK, ORBIT, PINK PEACE, ART & PROSE, WHORTLEBERRY SUMMER, STEELMOON Contests, and the Mid-Atlantic Horror Professionals website.

About the Island.

Tenerife, a Spanish island, is the largest (2034 sq. kms.) in the archipelago of the Canary Islands, with an estimated population of over 655,600 plus tourists. Its central mountain, Teide, stands at 12,200 feet, and is the highest in Spain. A cable-car ride to the summit offers unrivalled views of the lunar-like landscape of the volcanic slopes. The view from the peak is breathtaking. Colors from the different types of volcanic rock are seen clearly in hues of ochre, orange, and rust, green, black and beige, almost an entire color palette! On the higher slopes grow a variety of plants like the bushy clumps of Teide daisy flowers.

Like the rest of the Canary Islands, Tenerife is of volcanic origin. The last of the three eruptions that created the island happened about 3.5 million years ago, although small murmurs still occur. The most recent earthquake of about 4 on the Richter Scale was in 2002.

The northern coast of Tenerife is bordered by steep cliffs, but the southern part of the island slopes down to one of the few regions of level coastal plain in the volcanic islands of the archipelago. Tenerife has traditional rural towns, hillside villages and extraordinarily unusual landscapes formed from the twisted lava-rock of Mount Teide. It is indeed a paradise for tourists and makes an idyllic holiday destination.

According to some scientists the name Tenerife means snow-capped mountain in Guanche language. Tenerife is also referred as the island with two faces; an island with a 'north-south' divide, and a perfect climate with only very occasional rain. With lush forests (in the northern part), mountains, deserts, volcanoes, exotic plants and animal life, and spectacular beaches (with black volcanic sand), it's everyone's dream holiday place.

Published in the USA by **Whortleberry Press**
www.whortleberry.com

Printed in Great Britain
by Amazon